CONSTABLE IN THE COUNTRY

As he awaits his anticipated promotion, Constable Nick Rhea continues his work on the Yorkshire moorland beat of Aidensfield, reminiscing about his childhood in a similar idyllic village and making the inevitable comparisons. On his daily rounds he encounters an eccentric army of locals and visitors, none more so than Claude Jeremiah Greengrass, who splashes out on a colourful new car, only to have a pop group make him an offer he can't resist. The Beast of Aidensfield terrifies villagers by lurking in the darkness, and Constable Nick also has to deal with clever sheepdogs, psychic cows and ghostly racehorses...

CONSTABLE IN THE COUNTRY

Constable In The Country

by

Nicholas Rhea

Magna Large Print Books
Long Preston, North Yorkshire,
BD23 4ND, England.

British Library Cataloguing in Publication Data.

Rhea, Nicholas
Constable in the country.

A catalogue record of this book is
available from the British Library

ISBN   0-7505-2558-4

First published in Great Britain 2005 by Robert Hale Limited

Published in Large Print 2006 by arrangement with
Robert Hale Limited

Magna Large Print is an imprint of Library Magna Books Ltd.

Printed and bound in Great Britain by
T.J. (International) Ltd., Cornwall, PL28 8RW

Chapter 1

Having been born and reared deep in the countryside, I have spent most of my adult life working in blissful, even idyllic, rural surroundings. That is how it seems in comparison with the harshness of inner cities and depressed towns, or even when hearing of those who cope with a long daily trek to and from work in packed trains and on overcrowded roads. In my part of England, the roads are not congested; there are no inner-city type problems; there is very little crime and most of the people are utterly decent, charming and trustworthy. And although I live in North Yorkshire, I am not buried within an industrialized landscape, or lost in clouds of dense black smoke. On the contrary, I live in a landscape character-ized by wide-open spaces, fresh air, lush greenery, wild moors and birdsong.

North Yorkshire is not as some outsiders imagine, and the magnificent scenery shown in *Heartbeat* provides a colourful portrayal of but a very small part of our acres of wild beauty. North Yorkshire offers so much more, and it is South and West Yorkshire which have the industrial areas similar to those in the Midlands and Lancashire. They are a long way from the glories of the dramatic northerly portions of England's largest county, glories which include the Yorkshire Dales, the North York Moors and a spectacular coastline. And I must not ignore the East Riding with its delightful rolling uplands called The Wolds. That part of Yorkshire is dotted with pretty villages set around charming ponds, all with character-istics of their very own and quite distinct from other parts of the county.

I was born in a cottage in a quiet region of north-east Yorkshire described by Arthur Mee in his *The King's England* series, as being 'shut off from the world by the moors'. And so it was – we were in a deep dale surrounded by wild countryside of hills, heather, woods and rivers. My home was near the River Esk which carves its way through those hills and moors to empty itself into the North Sea at Whitby. With so much moorland – England's largest area of open heather in fact – and other wonderful scenery and pretty villages, few of us really appreciated the beauty and splendour of our very own part of England.

Nonetheless, we were clever enough not to tell everyone about it – we didn't want tourists, weekend visitors and incomers flocking in to drop their litter or block our roads with caravans. We didn't want them complaining about crowing cockerels or the lack of street lights; neither did we want them grumbling about rural smells and church bells. Then there are all those silly questions, such as 'Why was that church never finished?' (it was Whitby Abbey), or 'Do these villages have flushing toilets?' or 'Do you have electricity up here?'

Since my childhood, however, things have changed. Inevitably, word has reached people in other parts of the UK that the North York Moors provide a beautiful haven of peace and solitude. Or to be precise, that is how it used to be – for centuries, our moors echoed the famous words of St Aelred, the abbot of Rievaulx. In 1131, he said the district offered a marvellous freedom from the tumult of the world. Now, all that has changed. Farming and other rural occupations are in decline and tourism has become a big money-earner for Yorkshire folk. In these modern times, we have to tolerate the tourists with their litter, caravans and daft questions, but we swallow our pride as we take their money from them cheerfully. They have to pay to enjoy what is free for us canny Yorkshire folk!

There is no doubt that living in such a remote area has its benefits, but I'm sure some feel there are drawbacks or even hardships, but for me the thought of living in a town centre or suburbia, or even commuting to the town or suburbia for work, has never appealed in the slightest degree. I enjoy working from my home on the edge of the moors and perhaps this was bred into me because both my grandfathers worked from home – they kept pubs, one of which was also a farm – and my father also worked from home as a rural insurance agent. It seems to have become a family trait.

Life is made special by other factors too. For example, in many North Yorkshire villages there is a lack of pretentiousness as differing classes and professions mix cheerfully with one another. That is evident in the bars of Yorkshire village pubs where bricklayers, shop workers and farm labourers drink and chat with barristers, surgeons and top business people. Yorkshire village pubs cater for everyone, not cliques.

There are many other benefits such as quiet and pretty lanes, the ability to see the stars at night, the sounds, sights and smells of nature, the incredible views from local hilltops, the sheer expanse of purple heather on the moors in the autumn, and delightful villages which some might think have escaped the passage of time. There is all this plus the ability to freely explore and admire the beauty of the moors, dales, woods and river-sides. I could add lots of other bonuses, with some from my childhood days such as looking in nest boxes in the henhouse if we needed eggs; picking apples, pears and plums directly from the trees in our orchard, or collecting blackberries from the hedgerows and bilberries from the moors.

To feed our domestic fires, we gathered kindling and logs from the verges and woodlands (which I still do), and we would buy fresh potatoes or turnips by the sackful directly from the fields. Going into a shop to actually *buy* a pound of apples or a little bag of potatoes seems a very odd thing to do in the eyes of a lad reared with ample fruit and vegetable produce all around him. Another factor may be that my grandfather was a hunting, shooting and fishing person which meant that goodies like fresh rabbits, hares, pheasants, grouse and even salmon and trout were often on our menu – all free of charge, thanks to his efforts.

Perhaps due to the lack of monetary riches of many country people, most of the household maintenance was done by family members. Repairs, alterations, painting, decorating, plumbing, electrical work and so forth were all done by the man of the house.

Few in a village community would consider 'getting somebody in to fix it' because (a) it would cost money and (b) the man of the house could do it just as well and far more quickly. When the new, fashionable DIY arrived on the scene, it was regarded as a very weird concept by most country people who had been doing it all their lives because it was sensible, practical and necessary. And if they went into town to buy nails and screws, they did not come back with an ounce or two of each; they bought several pounds, enough to avoid the need for a repeat journey in the foreseeable future, say ten years or so. Large stocks of nails and screws – and almost anything else which was not perishable – made economic and practical sense. We still think like that. My garage, like those of my neighbours, is full of things which I am convinced will be useful at some date in the future.

In their sheds, those same country people

12

have a variety of tools which are capable of coping with anything from felling trees and cutting up timber to shaping stone, mending a leaking water pipe, installing shelves, painting and decorating, fixing electrical faults, pointing stonework, getting the car to start or making the clock tell the time. We believe everything comes in useful once every seven years even if it is merely a bit of rusty wire or some oddly shaped planks of wood. This rural abundance and self-sufficiency means that everyone, even the poorest, can still live very cheaply and comfortably in the great Yorkshire countryside.

It follows that being a village policeman living in a police house with an office attached was merely an extension of my earlier life, although I had completed four years on the beat in a small town to gain the necessary experience. Those years had taught me my craft and equipped me to work unsupervised on my own patch. Being trusted to work alone while making one's own decisions were the chief requisites for being in charge of a rural beat. One had to be relied upon to work efficiently, diligently and responsibly with a good practical knowledge of the law without a sergeant breathing down one's neck every minute of the day.

Being transferred to Aidensfield promised all those things I'd treasured and enjoyed in my formative years while offering the opportunity to test the various professional talents I'd developed during my early police career. I might also have to use the practical household skills I'd learned from my father, like doing all manner of jobs around the house. I was soon to discover, however, that I was not allowed to do simple things like renewing the washers on taps, or adjusting the toilet cisterns in the police house. A plumber had to be called in to such tasks because the property belonged to the police authority. I was not allowed to tamper with anything on the premises which meant it took ages for any minor defect to be repaired. I remember thinking I could have done many small maintenance jobs much more quickly and for a fraction of the eventual cost. A tap washer would have cost me two pence in old money, far cheaper than calling in a professional tradesman, but rules were rules and a plumber had to effect the repair even if the cost was far greater to the ratepayer.

If I had made such a repair, I would never have bothered to reclaim the cost of the washer – which made me think some aspects of life were, and still are, unnecessarily expensive, ponderous and bureaucratic. The solution was to effect such minor running repairs without telling anyone! Beyond doubt, the bureaucracy involved in doing it officially was an early job-creation scheme involving mountains of paperwork and undoubtedly a factor in causing monetary inflation. With my country-bred self-sufficient ways, I found this system very peculiar and most wasteful, albeit accepting that not every police officer could wield a hammer or operate a screwdriver.

On the whole, of course, there were massive benefits in living at Aidensfield. The police house was fairly remote which meant we had privacy and, of course, I worked from home. My children had the benefit of a rural upbringing with a good Catholic primary school and I was based in expansive countryside of the kind I remembered with pride and pleasure from my childhood. Some people would have paid a lot of money to live that kind of life. Furthermore, most of my work was out of doors and involved wonderful and interesting people, not to mention an endless variety of incidents and events. It was far better than work in a factory or office.

I was quite content that my children were being brought up near the purple moors with their never-ending views and it was re-assuring to know that the landscape in which we lived was full of real people, not to mention animals and birds, both wild and domestic. There was proper vegetation, too (not the dreadful artificial stuff I once saw on my family's only half-day visit to a But-lin's holiday camp); many of the plants provided food, and my children learnt that eggs didn't come from shops, but from hens. They saw that milk did not come from dairies, but from cows, and the food on our plates did not come out of a tin. Fires burnt logs and coal, not electricity or gas, and I was happy that my children learnt a lot about life in a very safe environment. I considered that vital in a fast-changing and rather uncertain world.

During my tour of duty at Aidensfield, it was inevitable I would look back upon the joys of my own childhood and compare them with our prevailing situation. It was also inevitable I would look and think ahead while trying to plan my four children's teenage years, their secondary education and possibly their university studies before wondering how each would earn his or her living. I'd always wanted to attend university but never had; I hoped my children would have the opportunity. Mary, my wife, might wish to resume her secretarial work, too. And, of course, there was my own career to consider. After a good deal of long and hard study, I had passed my promotion examinations which ensured I was qualified for higher rank. If I wanted to give my family the best I could offer within my range of skills, then promotion with its increased salary was important – but it would mean moving from Aidensfield. If I was promoted – and there was no guarantee that would happen – it was almost certain I would be transferred to a town where I would have to learn new responsibilities and a different way of living and working.

I would have to learn to cope with life and people in situations totally different from those to which I was accustomed. In my heart of hearts, I did not really want to work in a town although I recognized there might be merit in bringing up my family in a more thriving and cosmopolitan atmosphere. So was my happiness and contentment in Aidensfield important for us all? Or would the children benefit from a more sophisticated style of living? It was such thoughts which prompted these musings.

I began to doubt whether I could adapt to

an urban lifestyle. I knew how country people thought; I knew what made them tick, as people might say. I could identify birds, flowers and trees. I was accustomed to living in close proximity to livestock and knew the importance of the calendar in rural matters such as harvest-time or potato-picking. I knew what a grouse looked like, unlike one town-bred bobby who thought it was something like a rabbit. Another thought a handsome cock pheasant he'd seen on the roadside was something which had escaped from captivity, and yet another had no idea what a badger was. I could imagine such officers having difficulty with the poaching laws, wild-life protection and dealing with farmers, landowners and gamekeepers.

Then there was the woman who thought she could pop out and catch a bus at any time in Aidensfield. In fact our local bus ran only on Fridays, going to Ashfordly market and back again. She could not accept that such things actually happened, not when she came from London with buses and tube trains every few minutes. And the sound of an owl hooting at night caused terror in her soul.

I worked in a world far away from what some regarded as normal, but it was normal for me. And so, as I waited for the day I might wear three distinctive white stripes on the arm of my uniform tunic, I continued to work as the village constable of Aidensfield.

An example of town meeting country occurred when a farmer in remotest Shelvingby celebrated his hundredth birthday. At that time, it was a considerable achievement, even if a member of his family said he'd done nothing remarkable with his life except to grow old, adding he'd taken a mighty long time to do that. For the villagers, of course, it was an occasion worthy of celebration and it didn't take long for someone to offer to bake a cake and for someone else to suggest a party in the hall with everyone in the village being invited.

The old man in question was Frederick William Falkingbridge, known to all as Awd Fred, who had farmed at Ash Tree Farm. It was a very isolated spread in a tiny dale deep in the moors above the village and its only approach was by a rough track about a mile in length. The farm still belonged to his family and was now run by his grandson, Paul, and his wife June; Awd Fred lived in a modern bungalow built near the farmhouse where he was cared for by his son and daughter-in-law.

Awd Fred's son, Frank, and his wife Vera, were both in their seventies and had also retired from the farm, although Frank continued to work there whenever he was needed, usually at peak times such as harvest, haymaking, lambing, sheep-shearing or potato-picking. Both Awd Fred and Frank kept a close eye on Paul, although their shrewd advice, especially when buying and selling livestock, was valued. They all worked well together to maintain the farm which had been in the family for generations and the menfolk were particularly fortunate in their choice of wives. The ladies worked just as hard as their husbands in the family business and regarded it as a way of life rather than a mere job.

For anyone to reach the age of a hundred was unusual and it was thought Awd Fred was the only person to do so in the history of Shelvingby. Checks were made in parish registers and from elderly villagers, but no one could find another native centenarian in the village records. That fact provided an even greater reason for having a communal party with food, a bar, dancing and entertainment, and so the plans went ahead. Awd Fred and his family gave their approval. The celebrations would be in the village hall on the actual date of Fred's birthday which happened to be a Saturday. The party would start at 6 p.m. and finish at 11.45 p.m. as such events were obliged to do. The Sunday Observance Act of 1780, then in force, did not allow music and dancing on a Sunday in public places like village halls. This meant that the music, dancing and entertainment had to finish before midnight on the Saturday. Apart from that, it was felt Awd Fred might want to go home early anyway. Normally, he reckoned to be in bed before nine each evening but announced he had no objection to the party continuing in his absence.

I became involved because the organizers wanted to sell intoxicating liquor during the party and asked me about the procedure. I explained they would need to ask a local publican to supply the drinks, and he would then have to apply to the magistrates for what was known as an occasional licence. This would allow him to sell intoxicants away from his usual premises, i.e. in the village hall, and he would have to specify the hours required. It was a simple procedure and only twenty-four hours' notice was needed. The organizers had ample time to make that arrangement.

With such an important event on the horizon, it was inevitable the village newspaper correspondent would hear about it and she, being keen to earn a few shillings, sent notes to several local newspapers, including the *Yorkshire Post* in far-off Leeds. That prompted the paper's editor to despatch a photographer to take a few pictures of the grand old man while the local correspondent's words, plus a phone call to Awd Fred from a full-time journalist, would provide the necessary copy to accompany the chosen photograph. The photographer was a young woman called Felicity Ingram who had joined the *Yorkshire Post* from *The Birmingham Post* and who, being a woman in a man's world, was keen to show her prowess. She rang Paul Falkingbridge who was named as a contact because the old fellow didn't have a telephone. After explaining her purpose, Paul asked her to ring back in half-an-hour during which time he would fetch grandad into the farmhouse where she could discuss things with him in person. That would make Awd Fred feel really important.

The outcome was that Awd Fred agreed to have his photograph taken because he took the *Yorkshire Post* and liked the paper. He quite fancied himself on its news pages.

Felicity said she would drive out to Shelvingby on the Friday morning before his birthday. She promised to arrive around 11 a.m., saying the whole affair shouldn't take more than three-quarters of an hour. She could be back in Leeds in good time for the photograph to be processed for Saturday's edition which meant Fred's picture would appear on his actual birthday. On the preceding Thursday however, she rang Paul again. His father, Frank, happened to be in the house at the time, discussing the weekend's events.

'I'm sorry to trouble you, Mr Falkingbridge,' said Felicity. 'I can't find your farm on my road map. I've found the village but the farm isn't shown. Can you put me on the right road?'

'We're not on many road maps, Miss Ingram,' Paul explained. 'We're a mile up a private lane. Once you arrive at Shelvingby, take the first left after the shop, go through a white gate and follow the track for about a mile. If you get lost, ask at the shop, they'll put you right. You'll soon see our farm, it's high up on the hillside. We'll be waiting.'

'I can go and meet her,' offered Frank. 'She'll have to come through Aidensfield if she's coming from Leeds. Me and your mum allus go there on a Friday morning to the shop. If she parks outside the shop at half past ten, all she has to do is look out for my Landrover. She can't go wrong, there's only the one shop. Me and your mum have grey hair, tell her, we're old fogies. I'll flash my lights anyroad, and then she can follow us back here. That'll make it very simple for her. So what's she driving?'

Felicity had heard Franks remarks and thought it was a good idea; if she missed him in Aidensfield, she could always head for Shelvingby and ask the way, but Frank's offer was a bonus. She said she would look out for a green Landrover with a grey-haired man and woman on board, adding she would be driving a red Hillman Minx and that she was a blonde in her mid-thirties.

At 10.25 that Friday morning, knowing nothing of this arrangement, I happened to be outside Aidensfield Stores in uniform having just collected my morning papers. A clean red Hillman Minx arrived and eased to a halt, then a very pretty and smartly dressed young woman emerged and smiled at me.

'Hello, am I at the right place? This is Aidensfield, and this is the only shop?'

'It is,' I smiled. 'Right both times. Can I help?'

'Not really, I'm meeting someone here at half past ten and just made it. They've got a green Landrover.'

'Oh, well, there are quite a few of those hereabouts, but you've a few minutes yet.'

'I'd better get back into my car, I have to follow it from here and don't want to waste time.'

I walked back to my Mini-van which was parked on the road a few yards away and just as I was opening my driving door, I noticed the arrival of a green Landrover. It contained two people whom I did not recognize but I waved it past my van before I got in and the driver responded to my gesture by flashing his lights. He drove past me, turned left past the shop and headed out of the village.

The young woman in the red Hillman Minx then followed it. I was pleased her arrangement had worked so smoothly. I sat in my car for a few moments scanning the newspaper to check whether there was anything of particular interest to me in my work and then I noticed the arrival of the Falkingbridges' Landrover. It eased to a halt in front of the shop, Frank and his wife emerged and went into the premises. I thought nothing of it until I heard someone tapping on my van window a few minutes later. Frank Falkingbridge was standing outside so I climbed out for a chat.

'Morning, Frank.' I used his christian name even though he was old enough to be my father or even grandfather.

'How do, Nick. Did you see a young blonde out here just now, in a red Hillman? The lass in the shop reckons she saw it parked here.'

'Yes, she asked if this was the only shop in Aidensfield, because she was meeting someone here.'

'Aye, it's us,' he said. 'Me and the missus. That's who she's supposed to be meeting.'

'Well, she left only minutes ago....'

'Left? Where did she go?'

'I've no idea, Frank, she followed a Land-rover from here, and went that way,' and I pointed towards the western end of the village.

'It's my Landrover she's supposed to be following, not somebody else's!' he groaned. 'I was to flash my lights; I told her to look for two grey-haired old fogies.'

'Well, she's following somebody else right now,' I said. 'Do you want me to give chase? Is it important?'

'She's a photographer, coming to take

26

Dad's picture for the *Yorkshire Post*. I said I'd show her the way to our farm. So, who's she following?'

'Search me,' I had to say. 'I have no idea who it was. I've never seen them or their vehicle before; I don't think it was anyone local.'

'It's no good me giving chase, they could have turned off anywhere and with her right behind...'

'But she knows where you live?' I offered.

'Oh, aye, she's got our address and phone number, but because the farm's not on her map, she thought she might get lost so I said we'd be here at half ten and she could follow us up to the house. She's in a bit of a rush because she has to drive back to Leeds to get the photo processed for tomorrow's paper.'

'Well, at least you know she's in the area and not far away!' was all I could think of saying. 'She'll soon realize she's gone wrong and find her way there. Journalists and photographers are used to finding their way around strange areas.'

'Aye, you could be right. We'd best get back and hope she turns up.'

'I'm heading for Ashfordly,' I told him. 'I'll keep my eyes open for her and put her back on the right track if I find her.'

27

'Thanks, Nick,' he said, and returned to his vehicle. Although this was not a matter of life and death, I knew it was important for the Falkingbridge family and for Awd Fred in particular.

As I settled in my police van to drive into Ashfordly, I wondered how far that young woman would follow the wrong Landrover. Even if she was a stranger to the area, I felt sure she would quickly realize her mistake and head for Shelvingby. There were plenty of signposts indicating the route. When I arrived at Ashfordly Police Station, Alf Ventress was on duty in the office and speaking into the telephone.

As I entered, he interrupted his call while holding on to the handset and said, 'Ah, Nick, just the fellow. I've a job for you.' He then said into the phone, 'Just a moment, Mr Heslington, hang on a second or two, I've a constable here who will attend.'

Then he turned to me. 'Nick, this is a Mr Heslington on the line and he's ringing from High Barns Farm at Elsinby. He's there to look around as the place is for sale, but he says a strange woman has been following him and is now outside the house and won't go away. She keeps hammering on the door. He's locked himself inside, just in case she is dangerous. He's asked if we can help; he doesn't want to confront her or let her into the house.'

'If it's who I think it is, I'm sure she's not dangerous, but she's followed the wrong vehicle! I'll go straight out there, Alf it'll only take me fifteen minutes. Tell him to wait and do nothing till I get there.'

It was just after eleven when I arrived at High Barns Farm which had a 'For Sale' sign on the gate. It was not quite so remote as Ash Tree Farm at Shelvingby, but none-theless was half a mile or so from the nearest house. It had been for sale for some months and was unoccupied with no livestock on the premises.

The red Hillman Minx was in the foldyard and the blonde woman still walking around the house, knocking on the front and back doors and peering through the windows, desperately trying to make contact with the occupants. The green Landrover was parked nearby, but I could see no sign of its driver or anyone else. When she spotted my arrival, the blonde woman hurried towards me, recognizing me from our earlier meeting.

'Oh, Constable, I'm so glad you've come, I don't know what to do. I've been told to take photographs of an elderly gentleman and

they won't let me near him. I can't get anyone to answer my knocking. I know they're
in the house; I saw them go in. I've heard
country people can be a bit funny but–'

'I suspect you are at the wrong house,' I
interrupted her chatter. 'Am I right in
thinking you should be photographing old
Mr Falkingbridge?'

'Yes; I arranged with the family for them
to meet me in Aidensfield outside the shop,
in their Landrover. I was to look out for it
with two grey-haired people inside and they
would flash their lights at me, then guide me
to the farm because it's very remote and not
on my road map. I did that – and now this.
I ask you! Who do they think they are,
messing me about like this?'

'I'm afraid you've followed the wrong
Landrover and arrived at the wrong house,
this is High Barns Farm, Elsinby, not Ash
Tree Farm at Shelvingby. I'm here because
we've had a report of a suspicious character
making a nuisance of herself...'

'Suspicious? A nuisance? I'm just trying to
get somebody to answer the door, for God's
sake! I know they're in there.'

'Look, I'll lead you back to Shelvingby, to
the farm you should be visiting. We can take
a short cut along some back roads, but

before I go I'd better explain things to these people. For some reason, they didn't want to confront you. Look, go back to your car and turn it round, be ready to follow me out of here. Leave this bit to me, eh? And don't follow the wrong police van!'

'This must make me look a bit of a fool!' Realization of her mistake was now dawning and she forced a smile. 'They must think I'm mad.'

'Perhaps, but it makes me wonder why these people refused to answer the door to you!' I returned. 'I want to know why they're behaving like that, so make yourself scarce just now.'

I waited until the woman, whose name I did not know at that stage, had reached her Hillman and then I returned to the front door and hammered with the knocker. I guessed the inhabitants had been watching me and the blonde from the security of the house and after a while the door was opened by a man. He was very big in every sense of the word, tall, broad and muscular, and was dressed in a tweed suit. He had thick grey hair which I guessed was prematurely grey because he looked to be in his late forties.

'Mr Heslington?'

'Yes, and thank God you've come, Constable. I see you managed to chase off our trespasser. I don't want her in this house under any circumstances, or peering through windows. Is she a photographer?' He stared at the woman, now sitting in her Hillman some distance away and well out of ear-shot.

'As a matter of fact she is, but she's not interested in you.'

'You don't believe that, surely? Why else would she follow us here?'

I explained about Awd Fred's hundredth birthday and the photographer's real purpose, saying how she'd inadvertently followed the wrong Landrover and adding I would now escort her to the correct destination. I could see that he had misunderstood the entire situation even if his facial expression said he was not totally convinced by my version of the story.

'So why all this secrecy from you, Mr Heslington? People who want to buy farms don't usually react like this.'

'Oh, it's not me who's considering the purchase, Constable. Your colleague must have misunderstood me. I'm the agent who is acting for the vendor. My client is a lady who is inside right now, hiding from that photographer, not an easy job with no curtains at the windows. I fear we might now have lost the sale.'

'Because she doesn't like photographers?'

'Yes; when that woman started to follow us from Aidensfield we thought she was from one of the nationals and even though we tried to lose her in the lanes, she hung on. We managed to get indoors before she pulled up in the foldyard, but we daren't answer the door. My client wants privacy, you see, which is why she is considering this farm. I can't tell you her name, but she is very famous and often in the public eye, so the last thing she wants is her picture splashed all over the papers when she's looking for a bit of peace and quiet.'

'I can't tell the photographer that, can I? It'll only make her more determined to come back to see who's been viewing this place!'

'I'm sure you can think of a nice cover story for me, Constable, although I fear my client has rather been put off buying this farm. But thanks.'

When I returned to Felicity (later being told her name) sitting patiently in her car, I said that the man's wife was very nervous and neurotic, a former inmate in a mental hospital, and she thought she was being chased by one of the doctors from her unit, to have her returned. Felicity didn't know

33

whether to believe me or not. But it didn't matter because she'd lost interest in what might have been a very good story for her paper. She arrived at the Falkingbridges' farm about forty minutes later than planned and they laughed at her experience, but she assured Awd Fred there was still ample time to have his photograph taken and processed for tomorrow's edition.

Sadly, I never discovered who had been interested in High Barns Farm but the mysterious lady never went ahead with the purchase. Eventually, it was sold to a farmer who was not at all famous.

Chapter 2

Although most country lanes around Aidensfield were properly surfaced with tarmacadam, visitors from towns and cities were sometimes alarmed at their narrowness, frequent sharp bends and very steep gradients. Inclines of 1-in-3 (33%) were fairly common which caused great concern and even fear to drivers from the flatter areas of Britain, some of whom rarely coped with anything steeper than 1-in-20 (5%). Indeed, one of the fatal accidents with which I had to deal was that of a visiting gentleman from an area with few hills who probably lost his nerve when descending such a gradient. His car ran out of control and hit a tree, killing him and severely injuring his passenger. There was nothing wrong with his car – we tested it, paying particular attention to brakes and steering. No other vehicle or person was involved and the accident was surely due to him panicking at the unexpected severity of the gradient. I ought to add that there was a warning sign saying 'Steep Hill' on the approach, but perhaps he did not realize just how steep it was. I've known some drivers think hump-back bridges were steep hills.

Another problem was the variety of rural traffic which might be using the lanes. This could vary from a horse, with or without a rider, to a massive combine harvester which filled the carriageway, to the whole range of other rural inhabitants like dogs, pheasants, foxhunts complete with hounds, school nature walks with crocodiles of children, flocks of sheep, cows heading for the milking parlour or back to the fields afterwards, hikers, villagers, caravans, pedestrians of every kind including mums with prams and cyclists either in bunches or riding alone.

Then there are tractors, milk or petrol tankers, delivery vans, hedge-cutting machines, timber wagons, even lumbering badgers and children exploring. Wild wallabies have been spotted on our York-shire lanes too, and deer are quite common.

Country people appear to have no fear when using those lanes and they seem able to cope with anything they might encounter unexpectedly even when the carriageway appears too narrow for two vehicles to pass. A good country driver can squeeze a car through a gap of the kind one might consider only wide enough to accommodate a pedal cyclist, so it's not surprising that rural vehicles are often adorned with many dents and scratches. A tough hedge or lurking dry-stone wall – or even the horns of a stubborn cow and hoofs of a frisky horse – can quickly damage any car which ventures too close!

Furthermore, many visitors to our part of the world are not as skilled as their country cousins in evading the oncoming rustics and their accoutrements, so it's not surprising that some abruptly end their journeys in hedgebacks and ditches. In spite of this, serious collisions were surprisingly rare although demolished hedges and broken walls were a problem so far as straying livestock were concerned. Any herd or flock of livestock will find a hole in a fence within moments of it being created; they never miss such a good opportunity to take a walk to freedom. It is often wise to leave the offending vehicle *in situ* until the farmer can patch the hole, otherwise he might lose his cattle or sheep. Not many visitors appreciate that kind of logic.

Another problem is that some tourists and day-trippers seem to think open fields are nothing more than play areas for their dogs and children, or for having picnics, pitching tents, parking caravans and lighting fires. In their eyes, such open spaces are like town parks, there to be used by everyone. It is upsetting at times to learn how just rude or obnoxious some can be towards the farmers who own or work those fields. One mistaken but surprisingly common attitude was, and still is, that a field within a National Park is available for public use. Some townspeople still cannot differentiate between a National Park and a corporation or city park, failing to understand that most of the land within a National Park is privately owned and not open to the public.

An example of this occurred when an

Elsinby farmer called Terry Walsh found six people having a picnic in one of his fields. Terry owned Beckside Farm on the outskirts of Elsinby. It was not a hill farm of the moorland kind which specialized in sheep because it enjoyed a lowland riverside site with lush fields on either side of Elsinby Beck. Terry was a cattleman who was noted for breeding Friesians both for their beef and dairy products. He had a huge herd of the famous black and white cows, plus several bulls, and they could be seen dotted around his fields as they enjoyed the lush pastures. He had other stock too, including sheep and poultry, but the Beckside Herd of Friesians was his pride and joy and main source of income.

In his mid fifties, he was a sturdy man with a round, red face and brown eyes, who wore a flat cap, tweedy jacket, corduroy trousers and brown boots. He also had a delightful sense of humour. He looked like a typical countryman which, of course, he was, having spent his entire life on farms. A familiar sight around the district, he could often be seen visiting local marts and agricultural shows, and had found himself serving on a host of committees and panels where his wide knowledge of rural matters, his no-nonsense attitude to both authority and individuals, and his skill in countryside politics were extremely valuable.

On a fine, warm and sunny day in June, Terry was driving his car back from Ashfordly where he had attended a morning meeting in the Rural District Council offices. His route took him past one of his fields, known as the Hundred Acre, when he noticed the gate standing wide open. Thinking it was probably ramblers who had failed to secure it – even though it was not on a public footpath – he halted his car and went to close it. It was then that he noticed two cars parked in his field. Sitting on the grass near the vehicles were some people having a picnic. There were six adults in all, two men and four women, all middle-aged. They had lightweight chairs and table all set out with a cloth, food and drink and were clearly enjoying themselves. For a time, they were unaware of his presence as he walked towards them. They had selected a site about twenty yards into the field, fairly well away from the road on a downward-facing slope with a nice view of the stream below. As he approached, one of the women noticed him and alerted a man at her side. Terry heard him say, 'Leave this to me.'

The man then rose to his feet and waited for Terry to draw closer; the other man also rose. Both bore a look of menace and Terry sensed a confrontation of some kind, or at least some unpleasantness.

'Good afternoon,' he smiled. 'Have you permission to use this field?'

'What's it got to do with you?' The first man immediately adopted an aggressive stance. 'There's nothing here, the field's empty; it's not being used and the countryside belongs to us all.'

'I wouldn't agree with that because this is my field,' said Terry, without raising his voice. 'I'm a farmer; I work this land; it's part of my living.'

'And I work in a factory and where I come from we can use the park for picnics, and I believe – correct me if I am wrong – that this is within the National Park. That means it's for everybody.'

'I don't think you understand the purpose of the National Park. Most of it is private property, like this field,' pointed out Terry. 'This is not a city or town leisure park, and all I ask is–'

'Say what you like. We're having a picnic. We're doing no harm and there is nothing you can do to force us to leave. I know the laws about trespass: you can't throw us off; you can't touch us; you can only ask us to leave, and if you tell us to leave we shall do so when we've finished our purpose for being here.'

'That might be your decision, but I am now asking you to leave within the next fifteen minutes,' said Terry, his determination now operating at top gear. 'The time now is twelve-twenty.'

'I said we shall leave when we feel inclined, not when you dictate to us, I will not be dictated to by the land-owning classes,' the man said.

'Fifteen minutes,' said Terry.

The man ignored him. 'Come everybody, let's enjoy what's left of our picnic. This countryside buffoon can't make us leave; he has no powers and he knows it. The countryside's as much ours as his.'

He returned to his chair and made a great show of sitting down to continue his meal. Terry turned on his heel and left without more words, although he did have the wit to note the registration numbers of the two cars, just in case it became necessary to take this matter a stage further. His farmhouse was about half a mile from Hundred Acre field and he arrived to find his son removing his wellingtons outside the back door. He had come in from the other fields for the lunch Mrs Walsh was preparing in the farm kitchen.

Before he could get indoors, Terry said, 'I've a job for us, Alan, right now,' and he explained about the people in the field. 'This is what I want you and me to do; it'll only take twenty minutes or so.'

Fifteen minutes later, a herd of a hundred Friesians was being driven down the lane towards Hundred Acre field. Leading it was Terry on one tractor with his son Alan taking up the rear on another. The picnickers heard the tractors, but from their position inside the field, beyond a thick hedge and slightly down the slope, they could not see the oncoming cows. When Terry reached the gate, still open with the cars inside the field, he eased to a halt just beyond it and guided the leading animals inside.

The rest followed, bustling through the gate and bursting into the field as the startled people suddenly realized what was happening. The loud man leapt to his feet and shouted, 'Hey, you can't do this.'

'I can,' said Terry. 'It's my field, remember? I gave you a quarter of an hour to leave and you haven't. Time's up. You know the law, or so you said.'

And he shut the gate; then, before the trespassers could collect their picnic equipment and regain their cars, Terry had parked his tractor across the gateway and removed the ignition key, very effectively blocking the exit. There was no way they could remove the tractor and there was no other vehicular exit from the field. The cars were now trapped inside and the cows, as cows tend to do because they are very curious about all manner of things, ambled across to the picnic site and stood around in a huge circle, gazing at the scene. The women did not know whether to run for shelter in their cars or sit it out. They were not at all happy at being surrounded by a hundred cows or so.

'Come on, Alan,' said Terry. 'It's our dinnertime, we mustn't be late for that.'

'Hey, you, let us out ... you can't do this!'

'I just have!' laughed Terry.

He climbed aboard Alan's tractor and the pair of them chugged along the lane for their dinner, as the midday meal was known.

And that is when I became involved.

It was my day off duty and I was enjoying time in our garden with my wife and children later that afternoon when six people appeared at my gate.

One of the men, a forceful character and clearly the leader, came in and saw me sitting on the lawn with the children around me.

'Are you the policeman?' he demanded.

'Yes, I'm PC Rhea.'

'Well, you don't look like a policeman to me. You look as if you are skiving off work on a fine day.'

'It is my weekly rest day, sir; I am off duty. If you want a police officer, I suggest you ring Ashfordly Police Station from the kiosk in the village and someone will attend to you. If it's really urgent, or a matter of life and death, I am prepared to ring from here on your behalf. So what's the problem?'

'One of those land-owning bullies has locked my cars in his field.'

'Really? And how did that happen?'

'We were just having a picnic and this chap stormed in and tried to throw us out, so I stuck to my rights and said we were sitting tight till we'd finished ... men like him can't go bullying ordinary people like us, the land's for everyone. It's a free country.'

'So the owner saw you and asked you to leave?'

'Demanded we leave!'

'Did he use force?'

'No, he knew better than that. I'd have had

44

him by the short and curlies if he'd tried any funny business.'

'So he just asked you to leave?'

'He gave us fifteen minutes to get out, that's all.'

'You and your cars?'

'Yes, all of us, and our cars.'

'If he was the owner of the field, I'd say he was perfectly within his rights.'

'Now don't you start siding with him–'

'It's not a question of siding with anyone, it's a question of law. Are you saying you didn't leave when asked? So what happened?'

'He drove a herd of cows into the field and locked the gate, put a tractor across it.'

'So, now you will understand why he gave you fifteen minutes,' I said. 'Cows are moved quite regularly to allow the grass to grow in empty fields.'

'Look, are you going to do anything about this? You are the police constable, so you said.'

'I am not at work, sir. I am sure you don't work in your own time, so why do you expect me to?' I guessed he was a character of that kind of bloody-mindedness. 'But there is a more important point: what you have described is a civil trespass. If you did not have permission to go into that field,

45

you were trespassing on the farmer's land and he was quite within his rights to ask you to leave. Which he did, giving you ample time to comply and without using force. But you refused. You continued with the trespass, but trespass is not a matter for the police: it is a civil matter. There is nothing I can do; you must take up the matter with the farmer concerned.'

'All right, how about false imprisonment! I want to make a complaint about false imprisonment; he locked us in his field.'

'If you wish to pursue that course, sir, I cannot help as I am not on duty. If you care to wait, I will ring Ashfordly and have a constable attend to you as soon as possible. Perhaps you would care to wait on the village seat? Near the church?'

'Did you hear me? I said I want him arrested for false imprisonment!'

'Even though you are free? He did not lock you in the field, did he? He has not kidnapped you?'

'No, but he locked our cars in.'

'I doubt if any court would accept that cars can be subjected to false imprisonment or kidnapping, sir, and I would suggest he secured his gate to prevent you releasing his cattle and allowing them to stray. There is always a common law right to abate a nuisance too. Now perhaps you would listen to a word of caution. If you persist with these rather ludicrous complaints, you might find the farmer sends you a bill for car parking, and car parking in such a lovely place, a private field, can be fairly expensive...'

'Come on, Stan,' said one of the women, tugging his sleeve. 'You're making us all look idiots ... it was our fault, we should have asked, that's all. It costs nothing to ask, nothing to be polite.'

'Yes, but I don't like the ruling classes getting the better of me.'

'Can I make a suggestion?' I asked.

'Please,' said the woman who had spoken. 'All I want to do is to get home now.'

'You should go and apologize to the farmer,' I suggested. 'I am sure he'll release your vehicles. And I would think nothing more will be said.'

'I can't do that! I can't lower myself to grovelling in front of a landowner to get my own car back!'

At that stage, the second man stepped forward and took Stan's arm. 'Come on, Stan, you've made your point. If you won't apologize to the farmer, then I will; we're the ones at fault. You wouldn't want him parking his tractor in your garden, would you? Have you any idea who the farmer is, Constable?'

I asked him to describe the field and its whereabouts, and then realized it belonged to Terry Walsh, and told them how to locate his farm. The people said they would walk back together to find the farm and, with the exception of Stan, said they would present themselves together to make the apology, even if Stan refused. And off they went. It was quite a long walk, a good half-hour.

I rang Terry to warn him of the impending arrival of the little group and he thanked me, then told me the full story. 'I'll let them get their cars out if that clown apologizes. You know, Nick, if only they'd asked me, they could have stayed there as long as they wanted. I just hope that chap has learned something from this.'

'I doubt it,' I felt compelled to say. 'His sort never learn.'

If that story involved a herd of cows, albeit not upon the road, there was another seasonal problem on the lanes. It was mud. Loads of it in thick, sticky layers and lumps all over the road surface. In the autumn and early winter, there was always a lot of activity in the fields due to ploughing, harvesting the

48

potato crop, repairing hedges, clearing ditches and generally preparing the land for the coming year's harvests. That kind of work required the presence of vehicles on the wet and soggy land and when they left the fields to return home, they deposited layers of mud, earth, dirt and other filth on the road surfaces. There were times it was difficult to see the solid tarmac surface beneath the layers of filth and in some cases, mud might be spread from several fields over a considerable distance, a mile or more in some cases. Lots of lanes reverted to the appearance they must have had long before John Loudon Macadam (1756–1836) produced the idea of using crushed stone for road surfaces. I've known occasions when some lanes had a layer of almost three inches of thick, sticky brown mud.

The prevention of that condition was far from easy. Farmers must work their land and when they do, it is inevitable that mud and dirt is deposited on the roads, but the problem is not particularly one of unsightliness. Rather, it is a case of possible danger to other road users. If the mud is wet, it is slippery too, which means vehicles can skid when cornering or braking, but when the mud is frozen, striking a lump with a wheel is tantamount to running into a brick. It follows there was great danger to two-wheeled vehicles, especially fast-moving motor cycles but one could not ignore the risks to horses and their riders too, or even pedestrians.

Not surprisingly, the law tried to deal with the problem. In some parts of the country, byelaws attempted to prevent mud being deposited on public roads, but because their penalties were a maximum of a £5 fine, lots of farmers ignored them. It was often considered worth risking a fiver to get their work completed on time; consequently, most of these byelaws were toothless tigers.

I never knew an occasion where a byelaw was used in such a case. Instead, most police forces relied on the spirit of the old Highways Acts whose provisions had been modernized and consolidated in the comparatively recent Highways Act of 1959. Section 140 said it was an offence if a person, without lawful authority or excuse, deposited anything whatsoever on a highway in consequence whereof a user of the highway was injured or endangered. The snag with this legislation was that it was never easy to prove that a farmer had endangered anyone unless there was an accident of some kind, and furthermore, he could claim the mud was there through a lawful excuse, i.e. that he was working in his fields. If someone was actually injured, it was easier to prosecute an offender, but the overall effect was that farmers would erect signs near their fields saying *Danger – Mud on Road* and thus avoid prosecution. They would argue they had taken all reasonable steps to warn road users of any danger from mud-covered roads, and they always said they cleared the mud at the first opportunity. If someone was injured, it was amazing how many times it happened as the farmer was actually working in the fields, i.e. before he had had time to clean the road. The police, on the other hand, would threaten careless farmers with prosecution if mud was seen on a road without such a warning sign.

In most cases, they would tell the farmer to get the road cleaned without delay, otherwise he might face prosecution; if he complied there would be not be a court case and that was usually a good compromise. In short, mud on the road was one of those ongoing rural problems with the police constantly nattering at farmers, the driving public constantly nattering at the police and the farmers always nattering that it took precious time and money to keep the roads clear of mud. They maintained that if people knew there was mud on the road, they would take care when driving or riding. Most farmers and landowners though were highly responsible people who did their best to minimize that kind of danger.

One exception was Dick Middleton of Cragside Farm, Whemmelby. He was approaching eighty years of age and still working during my time at Aidensfield, but he recalled the days when the lanes around his village were not surfaced with tarmacadam. They were little more than mud tracks littered with underground rocks and riddled with deep potholes. In his view, lumps and layers of mud on a modern road surface were nothing to grumble about – when he was a lad, all roads were like that and folks had no trouble with them. He could not appreciate that modern traffic moved at a far greater speed than in his youth so he reckoned any driver should be able to cope with a muddy surface. Certainly, all the local people were aware of his propensity for leaving mud and the local police regularly warned him to clean up after his tractor had passed. In spite of this proclivity, he was never prosecuted, chiefly because no one had been hurt due to the deposits of mud he left behind.

And then one December morning a traffic accident occurred on a stretch of road between Dick's fields and Whemmelby village. A motor cyclist, a stranger to the area, was chugging along the lane towards Whemmelby. When he rounded a sharp corner, he was confronted by a sea of mud across the entire width of the carriageway. It had been carried in repeated journeys from a nearby field and covered the whole road surface, but the snag was that it was frozen. The front wheel of the motor bike hit a lump of frozen mud which was like colliding with a half-buried upright brick. It threw the bike off course with the result that the rider crashed through the hedge, fell off and landed unceremoniously in Dick's field. Dick had been working that field the previous day and had not cleaned the road surface after himself; there had been a severe overnight frost which covered the road surface with lumps of frozen mud. It was highly dangerous as this unfortunate man had discovered. Happily, he was not injured, although his bike suffered minor damage, so he came to me to report the accident. His bike was in a rideable condition.

The rider was Hugh Evans who came from

Leeds and was touring the area, taking photographs and undertaking research for a holiday feature in a magazine. He grumbled that his camera had been smashed in the accident, but happily he was insured. As I took details, he stressed that his mishap had occurred solely due to the thick layer of frozen mud which covered the road surface, in particular one frozen lump which had protruded higher than the rest to cause his mishap. He added there was no warning sign from the farmer. He said he wanted to record those facts because his insurance company would require that information; he intended making a claim from the farmer for the damage to his camera and his motor bike, adding he was more concerned about his camera because it had contained some used film. His work to date would probably be ruined, so he asked for the farmer's name.

From the location given to me by Mr Evans, I knew it was Dick Middleton and provided his details. Mr Evans then asked if Dick would be prosecuted and made it clear that he felt such a course was inevitable. Mr Middleton had caused danger to a road user by not clearing the mud from the road and, of course, a successful prosecution would help his insurance claim. I told him the matter would rest with my superiors but certainly it would be considered; it was my task to submit a factual report about the entire incident, I then advised him that his insurers should write to my force to request an abstract of the accident report, and off he went. My next task was to visit the scene.

When I arrived, the road was thick with mud which had melted in the morning sunshine, for the night frost had disappeared as the sun rose. Even in its liquid state, I could see the mud was lethal to a motor bike; a horse might slip too, and if there had been frozen chunks, a horse could stumble over one of them and break a leg. I went to see Dick, told him about the accident and warned him to get the road cleaned. He told me he had tried the previous night but it had frozen solid by the time he'd got around to it, but he said he would now finish the task because the sun had softened it.

I warned him he could expect to be prosecuted once my bosses studied the accident report. My report then had to pass through several superior officers, beginning with the sergeant at Ashfordly, proceeding through the hands of the inspector at Eltering to eventually arrive on the superintendent's desk at Divisional Headquarters. It was from there that eventually I received a memo instructing me to visit Dick Middleton to inform him he would be prosecuted for depositing mud on the road in consequence whereof other road users were endangered. A summons would be issued in due course.

Dick was a small, active man with a ginger moustache, thinning ginger hair and rather bulbous eyes behind thick spectacles, and when I told him the purpose of this visit, he said, 'Aye, well, Mr Rhea. I'm right sorry about it, and I know you have to do your job, but it was definitely frozen when I tried to shift it, so I couldn't move it. It was rock solid. Then that morning it was all soft again but that feller came across it before I had chance to get it cleaned up... I'm not as wick as I was, you know, not at my age...'

The outcome was that Dick appeared before Ashfordly Magistrates' Court charged with an offence under section 140 of the Highways Act, 1959. Much to everyone's surprise, he pleaded not guilty which was why he had to appear before the bench. Had he pleaded guilty, the case could have been dealt with in his absence. He had asked advice from his National Farmers' Union representative and they had appointed a defence solicitor.

It was the practice of that NFU man to always plead not guilty on the grounds that the court might find some element of doubt in the prosecution's case and so return a verdict of not guilty. That would then mean the NFU might not have to pay compensation or meet insurance claims. That representative was sitting beside Dick in court; his name was Graham Newberry.

The motor cyclist, Hugh Evans, gave his version of events and was cross examined by Mr Newberry. Even then, I could see doubts beginning to creep into the magistrates' minds because Newberry suggested Evans had not collided with a lump of frozen mud but may have hit something else, like a stone, which had not been left there by Dick Middleton. In the glare of the courtroom, Evans admitted that might be the case; he had not actually seen what his front wheel had struck, although frozen mud was the most likely explanation. And, of course, he'd not been able to take a photograph of the offending lump because his camera had been damaged.

I then gave evidence about visiting the scene shortly after Mr Evans's accident and recording the condition of the road, i.e. that it was covered with a thick layer of mud.

Under cross examination by Mr Newberry, I said the mud was not frozen at the time of my visit, adding that I did not know whether it had been frozen at the time of Mr Evans's mishap. I agreed that even in December, sunshine could melt frozen ice very quickly and so the mud could have been frozen earlier but had softened very speedily before my inspection. This meant I had been unable to find the piece of mud which had caused the accident, although I stated that in my opinion the condition of the road was such that it would present danger to any unwary motorist whether frozen or not. Mr Newberry then raised the possibility that the motor cyclist may not have been driving with due care and attention, and then, having planted that seed of doubt, he announced that his client, Dick Middleton, would go into the witness box. He was not obliged to, but both Mr Middleton and Mr Newberry felt it would be in the interests of justice for him to present his own version of events. He was first examined by Inspector Harry Breckon who was prosecuting in the absence of Sergeant Craddock who was on leave. Having established that Dick Middleton was owner of the field in question, and that he had been working in that field the day prior to the accident, and that his tractor had dropped a lot of mud on the road, some of which was in the form of lumps, the inspector asked, 'So, Mr Middleton, you agree your tractor deposited lumps of mud on the road after you'd been working in your fields?'

'Aye.'

'How big were those lumps?'

'Middlin'.'

'So how big is middlin'?'

'A fairish size.'

'So is a fairish size large or small?'

'Whey, it's sort of neither big nor small, middlin' like I said.'

'So middlin' is about the same as fairish?'

'Aye.'

'I am still not sure how big those lumps were. So if I was to ask you to compare the size of those lumps with something else, how would you then describe them?'

'Whey, I'd say each was about as big as a stone.'

'What size of stone?'

'I'd say a middlin' sort of stone, a fairish one.'

'Not a small stone?'

'It all depends on what you mean by small, Inspector. There's small and little, tiny and not so big, and very small like gravel, but I'd say my lumps were a bit bigger than that but not as big as dry-stone walling stones but bigger than bits of gravel or little pebbles, although they might be about the size of a fairish bit of gravel but I did go out that night to try and shift them, however middlin' they were, but they were frozen solid. There was nowt I could do to shift 'em.'

At this point, the chairman of the bench interrupted. 'Inspector and Mr Newberry, I think it has been established that the defendant was responsible for depositing mud on the road in question, and it has also been established that Mr Evans fell from his motor cycle in circumstances which may or may not have been due to that mud. However, the mud was on the road at the time of the accident, that is not in dispute.'

'Yes, Your Worship,' muttered Inspector Breckon.

The chairman continued, 'Now, Mr Newberry, are there any final questions you wish to put to the defendant?'

'No, Your Worship. All I wish to say now is that the defendant admits there was mud on the road at the time of Mr Evans's accident, and that he was responsible for that mud being there. He had earlier tried to remove it but a severe frost made it impossible. However, it is submitted that the mud was not likely to cause a user of the highway to be endangered or injured if he or she took due care when driving or riding. However, the prosecution has not established that Mr Evans's motor cycle actually struck a piece of frozen mud left there by Mr Middleton. The constable did not find any such frozen lump when he visited the scene soon after the accident. Mr Middleton could have struck some other object which has not been found. On those grounds, I submit that my client is not guilty as charged.'

'We shall adjourn for a few moments to consider the verdict,' said the chairman, and the bench of three then rose and left the courtroom.

As we all waited, Inspector Breckon approached me with a wry smile on his face. 'The fact is, PC Rhea, that Dick Middleton left a lot of mud on that road, and a motor cyclist came to grief because of it. That's all we need for a conviction. But you know what rural magistrates are...'

After a few minutes, the door of the meeting room opened and an usher shouted, 'The court will rise' and we all stood as the magistrates returned to their seats.

'Mr Middleton,' the chairman addressed Dick, who was standing in the floor of the court, cap in hand, 'we have considered the evidence in this case and conclude that you did deposit undue amounts of mud on the highway in question and we accept that it contributed in some way to Mr Evans's accident. However, in view of the circumstances, the frosty evening for example, which meant you could not clear the road in spite of trying and the fact there is no evidence that Mr Evans actually struck a piece of frozen mud, we have decided to give you an absolute discharge. You are free to leave the court.'

There were sighs of relief all round, but Inspector Breckon came over to me and said, 'A good and sympathetic verdict, PC Rhea. Not many people realize that an absolute discharge is a conviction – but one with no penalty.'

'I wonder what the insurance companies will make of that?' I asked.

'One may not doubt that, somehow, good shall come of water and mud,' he smiled. 'Rupert Brooke wrote that, whatever it means.'

'Really, sir,' was all I could think of saying.

Chapter 3

During their years of service, police officers can expect to deal with a variety of sexual offenders. Throughout history, rape has undoubtedly been the worst of the sexual crimes due to the physical violence which is often involved. Not surprisingly, the crime carried life imprisonment under the Sexual Offences Act of 1956. The high degree of emotional trauma suffered by the victims did not feature in the statute and that aspect of the crime was sometimes overlooked by the courts. They dealt dispassionately with facts which had to be either proved or disproved, and in trials of suspected rapists innocent women victims were often made to appear as prostitutes or women of loose morals. Credibility of the victim's story was always a major factor at a rape trial, and some behavioural trait, such as a woman not making an outcry at the time, or even wearing a short skirt, could appear to suggest she was not telling the truth, i.e. that the rape was a false allegation. Some women, after being raped, would hurry home and have a bath before mentioning it to anyone – sadly, that was always a point in favour of the accused's statement that his victim had consented. An immediate or early report, and an outcry, was considered good evidence that such a crime had been committed.

The defence counsels of some suspected rapists cruelly demolished the evidence of innocent and traumatized victims, so it is not surprising that few women reported this most dreadful of crimes. Not many could face the ordeal of appearing in court where their private lives were revealed to a salacious public, while another factor was that many rapes were committed by a man known to the victim. Sadly, the word of one woman against a rapist was usually insufficient to secure a conviction or even a prosecution – the law required some form of corroboration of her account, either from another witness, or perhaps in the form of other evidence, usually scientific. Such supporting evidence was not always available.

In addition to rape, there was a wide range of other sexual offences in the 1960s, most carrying lesser penalties. They included sexual intercourse with girls who were under sixteen, (albeit made more serious and tantamount to rape if the girl was under thirteen), intercourse with women who were mentally defective, indecent assault, incest, prostitution in all its forms, procuration, abduction of females, gross indecency, indecent language, advertisements, exhibitions and publications, indecency with children (not then considered particularly serious) and a collection of unmentionable and ill-defined offences grouped under the heading of 'unnatural crimes', some of which involved animals while others involved only men. Similar offences involving women only, i.e. lesbians, were not illegal because it was claimed that Queen Victoria refused to approve the necessary section in the Offences Against the Person Act of 1861. She refused to believe that women behaved in such a way.

Both male and female police officers investigated and dealt with sexual cases although where women and young children were involved, and where it was necessary for a sensitive and sympathetic approach, it was normal practice for women police officers to interview the victims and then conduct the case to its conclusion. Indeed, police women of all ranks became experts in dealing with that very specialized aspect of criminal investigation.

So far as rural constables were concerned, the most serious of these crimes were rarely committed upon their beats. During my time at Aidensfield, for example, there was only one reported rape on my patch, but it was later discovered the woman had consented to what took place. False accusations of that kind were not unusual. There were no reported indecent assaults and none of the other crimes such as prostitution, procuration and abduction. I think it is fair to place on record that offences like indecent assault, sexual intercourse with girls who were under sixteen, incest and even some 'unnatural crimes' did take place in both urban and rural areas and it was inevitable that some occurred on my patch, but very few, if any, were reported to the police. In the phraseology of the time, details of such delicate matters were often kept 'within the family'. Many people thought that some things were best left 'unsaid' even though the police believed that the most common crime in England was incest. Very rarely did anyone report such a thing to the police – honour or sheer embarrassment exercised a strong influence over family members no matter how evil, deranged, sad or ignorant they were. In fact, a surprising number did not consider incest to be a criminal offence.

For all the seriousness of sexual offences, there was one which, in many instances, caused hilarity, albeit that some victims could be frightened, upset, traumatized and angry, in many instances the intended targets were amused or baffled by the actions of the offender. Indeed, the finest punishment he could receive was for his victims to laugh at him, or pour scorn either upon his behaviour or upon that part of his anatomy which was the focus of attention. I am, of course, referring to that odd group of men known as flashers. The formal name for the offence is indecent exposure. What compels a man to deliberately display his private parts to selected victims by opening his flies or flinging open the skirts of a dirty macintosh is something which has long puzzled psychiatrists and police officers.

During the 1960s, it was surprisingly prevalent across Britain with flashers being hard at work in parks, formal gardens, woodlands, beaches, hotel bedrooms overlooking the street, private gardens, picnic sites and places to which the public had access such as York City Walls, ruined abbeys, double-decker buses and sports fields; almost any place of public resort could expect a visit from a flasher at fairly regular intervals. Some flashers operated in secret, revealing their splendour only to a selected victim whom they knew would be passing a certain point at a particular time. I recall one who performed regularly near the City Walls at York under cover of the dark evenings as female staff from a nearby office were leaving for home. His displays, always in the light of a convenient street lamp, did not last for many days because the girls laughed at him and some even tried to take flash photographs, so he gave up. That middle-aged man was never found and his identity was never known. One of the victims – or perhaps we might say one of his audience – told me it was not easy to remember his face when the man in question was determined to render some other part of his body distinctly unforgettable.

It was during the autumn and early winter of one year that a flasher began to display his wares at the bus station in Ashfordly. It is by no means certain when he started because the police felt he had been entertaining the uncomplaining home-bound bus queues for some time before his activities became known to us. Once we received a formal complaint, however, we had to take appropriate action which meant obtaining a description of him, circulating it to local constables in the hope of obtaining his name and address, and then maintaining observations with the intention of catching him in action.

It soon became clear that he operated around five o'clock in the evening when it was dark, the only illumination coming from some rather dim bus-station lights. That was when queues of office secretaries and other staff, almost all female, were waiting for their buses home. It also became evident that he operated only when it was foggy. A combination of darkness and fog meant that only those very close to him were treated to a grandstand view; he could target his audience and then vanish into the gloom before anyone could catch him. No one chased him or tried to follow him because they had buses to catch – all they wanted was to get home.

His *modus operandi* was very simple. From the witness statements we gathered, we knew he operated between 5.00 and 5.30 on certain evenings, Monday to Friday, although no particular evening was preferred. To our knowledge, he had never appeared at a weekend. On the occasions we knew about, he had been seen on weekday evenings without any more detailed pattern emerging, except that he always operated within the same half-hour. Similarly, his manifestations were always within the same small area of the bus station. With one exception, he had always been spotted near the Elsinby queue. On that solitary exception, the night had been extremely foggy and we wondered if he had got lost so that he flashed at some other bus queue. We learned that two buses left for Elsinby, one at 5.05 p.m. and the other at 5.35 p.m, so he had a captive audience during any workday evening; on Saturdays, of course, most of the office staff finished at lunchtime and we'd had no reports of a daytime flasher.

It was while taking a look at the bus station that I realized the toilets were very close to the platform where the Elsinby queues gathered each evening. Not only that, the toilets had been constructed fairly recently. They formed an extension to the existing waiting-room with access from both inside and outside but the important thing from my point of view was the narrow gap between the waiting-room and that toilet block. The toilets, incidentally, comprised both ladies' and gents'. The gap between the buildings was only some four feet wide by about eight feet deep with a roof, ideal for sheltering a few pedal cycles if you worked at the bus station. At night, however, it was dark inside that small space and inevitably the floor was covered with rubbish which was either thrown in or blown in, and beneath the clutter was an inspection chamber for drains. That was why it had not been built upon. That little space, a handy shelter in bad weather, made a very useful hiding place, especially in fog. I thought it was perfect for a man who wanted to leap out to surprise or impress people with a display of his manly tackle.

Because the alley was so close to the toilets, I was unsure whether he went in there first, perhaps to remove his daily clothes and change into his working uniform of naked skin and raincoat. Alternatively he could have walked through the streets already attired for action. If that was the case, he probably lived nearby and used the fog to conceal his journeys. Certainly it would be cold if he was clad in just an old raincoat, another reason for thinking he lived nearby, although the weather would never defeat a truly determined street entertainer. I began to think he lived close, somewhere convenient for a dash across the street while wearing very little – and, being local, he would know his way around in dense fog. My sneaking suspicion was that when he vanished in the fog, he went straight home although it was possible he hid in the toilet for a while. He could have concealed another coat inside the gents' toilet, or even concealed one beneath that whose flaps he opened with such anticipated dramatic effect. If he had done either of those things, he could make a rapid change of clothing before emerging to stroll home in a new disguise, feeling he had done another good day's work. A hat of some kind would complete his disguise – he always flashed with his head and everything else bare. But those thoughts were all speculation.

Over the weeks, we attempted to keep observations on the bus station between the relevant times, but we did not have the manpower or the time to be there every evening, nor could we know in advance when it was going to be foggy. It was sod's law that he would appear on the very night we could not attend, so perhaps he was watching for signs of a police presence? We felt that was unlikely because it was probable he would not realize his activities had been reported to us; we had not identified him which meant he had not been interviewed, and nothing of his endeavours had reached the local newspaper. There was no reason for him to know we were trying to catch him – indeed, he might not even realize he was breaking the law. Quite a lot of people who had witnessed him in action did not consider him a law-breaker. They just thought he was barmy, little more than a nuisance. I don't think anyone thought he was dangerous.

We became increasingly convinced he lived nearby because he always arrived while it was foggy. We felt he must know when the bus station was shrouded in fog because that was a vital element of his activities. Fog can suddenly clear too, so he needed to live close enough to disappear indoors if that happened. The fact he must be very local meant he would recognize any of the Ashfordly police officers who might be keeping observation in plain clothes, and he might even spot any off-duty police officer who happened to be waiting for a bus. That sort of thing would deter him and could mean we might never catch him.

Over the weeks, his performances con-tinued spasmodically and we felt he was still in blissful ignorance of our professional interest in his displays. Thus it remained possible to lay a trap and arrest him. The longer he operated without restriction, the more daring – and careless – he would become. After consultations with the CID at our Sub-Divisional Headquarters and because he seemed to be getting increasingly active and some women were now beginning to express fear and alarm, it was decided to plant an undercover police officer in the Elsinby bus queue.

A 30-year-old policewoman in plain clothes, dressed to look like an office worker, would join the queue and remain at the bus station between five o'clock and six o'clock each weekday evening during the first week in November. Fog was almost guaranteed on one or more of those evenings. Regrettably, it was decided that she could not have the back-up of a local male officer because it was felt he might be recognized; if the flasher spotted him, there would be no gala performance.

The policewoman, Detective WPC Angela Griffiths was a former athlete whose skills ranged from sprinting to javelin throwing, who joined us from the CID in Scarborough, some thirty miles away, who therefore wouldn't be recognized in Ashfordly. If the flasher was not apprehended during the first week, she would do the same thing the following week and even the one after that. We were aware he might realize there was a new face in the bus queue, but if the same woman appeared each evening for three weeks, he might think she was a new member of staff in one of the town's offices or shops. Angela had been given a good description of the flasher; it was a composite picture provided by several reliable witnesses, and most importantly, she knew the colour and style of his old raincoat. That was his working dress because he'd worn it on every occasion. And so the trap was set.

It is one of those unfortunate certainties that on such occasions the best laid plans never seem to produce the desired result. In this case, during the first week of that vigil, the flasher did not make a single appearance, even though four of the evenings were foggy.

On the second week, all the evenings were crisp and clear; as expected, he did not appear. Likewise he did not turn up on the first Monday of the final week of the planned observation and, by now, the detective inspector at Divisional Headquarters was getting rather restless. He felt that his policewoman detective had better things to do in Scarborough where more serious matters required her attention. It seemed the entire project was going to be a waste of time, but because he had promised her services for three full weeks, her boss grudgingly agreed to let her continue until that Friday. If nothing happened by then, she would be withdrawn.

On that final Tuesday, she struck oil. Or rather, she struck something else.

As the queue waited patiently for the 5.35 to Elsinby in thick fog, the flasher suddenly appeared on the tarmac moments before it would be used by the incoming bus. He shouted some incomprehensible words to draw attention to himself, threw open his old raincoat and exposed what the legislators described as 'his person' which was erect. The legislators of that time rarely called rude things by their real names – for example, in section 78 of the Highway Act of 1835, it created an offence *if the driver of any carriage on the highway quit the same and went to the other side of the highway fence*. It was no more specific than that. In the days before public lavatories, that was one way a coachman could relieve himself on a long journey, but our lawmakers were rather delicate when referring to such matters. Likewise, when it came to indecent exposure by men, the

Vagrancy Act of 1824 said it was an offence wilfully, openly, lewdly and obscenely for a man to expose his naked person with intent to insult any female. Even if the legislators did not specify exactly what this meant, subsequent prosecutions established precisely what it was. Most of us knew it wasn't something like a bare knee or hairy chest.

On that night, therefore, a woman in the queue screamed as Angela Griffiths sprang into action. The flasher was momentarily stunned by this unexpected development because he stood still long enough for her to reach him and seize the sleeve of his old coat. But, like an eel, he slipped it off and began to run, stark naked, into the safety of the dense fog. But Angela's athletic prowess had not deserted her and she gave chase and caught him. She managed to hold on to him until they reached Ashfordly Police Station where he was charged with indecent exposure, contrary to Common Law. His old raincoat was later recovered at the scene and kept as evidence.

The man's name was Clarence Mason, an unmarried 50-year-old tailor who worked for himself in a tiny shop near the town centre. He lived above the premises which was only a couple of minutes from the bus station and he regularly closed his shop at five o'clock. He never provided any explanation for his bizarre behaviour, but when he appeared before Ashfordly Magistrates' Court, other witnesses told their story and finally Angela gave her evidence with all the confidence of an experienced detective. Their Worships listened with every inch of concentration they could muster, and then the chairman asked, 'Detective Constable Griffiths, you say the defendant had discarded his raincoat and was completely naked when you arrested him. Might I ask how you managed to maintain a grip upon him in those circumstances?'

'I seized what the law refers to as his person, Your Worship. It meant I had no difficulty persuading him to accompany me to the police station.'

'That is perfectly understandable.' And then the chairman turned to the defendant. 'Mr Mason, as a former law-abiding and respected resident of this town, you have made a complete fool of yourself while alarming members of the public. However, as this is your first offence, I have no hesitation in granting you a conditional discharge, the condition being that you do not repeat this behaviour for the next three years. If you do, you will go to prison. We need to keep our town free from the activities of such people.'

And so the phantom fog flasher of Ashfordly was brought to justice. Angela, being a former javelin thrower, had a strong grip and local police lore says the flasher had tears in his eyes as she propelled him towards the police station.

One of the odd aspects of the law which was used to deal with Clarence Mason was that it referred only to men. It contained no provision for women who might indecently expose 'their persons'. This is the wording of section 4 of the Vagrancy Act of 1824 – *It is a summary offence for any person wilfully, openly, lewdly and obscenely to expose his person with intent to insult a female*. It might be argued that the term *any person* could include a woman, and that the word *his* in law, might also include *her*. There is an old saying in law which said that *In English law, male embraces female* but in this instance, the statute does refer to the intent to insult a female, implying the offender must be male.

So what was the situation if complaints were received about a woman behaving indecently? One resort was section 28 of the

Town Police Clauses Act of 1847 which said, 'It is a summary offence wilfully and indecently to expose the person in any street in any urban district (where the Act is in force), to the annoyance of residents or passengers, and the offender may be arrested without warrant.' Clearly, this caters for male and female offenders, but the Town Police Clauses Act was not in force in rural areas which meant it could not be utilized in the countryside.

Indeed, it was not in force throughout the whole of England and Wales, but only in those towns which had adopted that statute. Readers will also note that it related only to *any street* and that raised the question of whether flashers broke that law if they performed in parks and gardens, on buses or trains or anywhere which was not a street. In such cases, there was a further provision for us to fall back upon – common law. Common law was wonderful because it catered for crimes and offences which were not written down in statute form and it did not rely on precise wording.

Rather, it depended on common sense and in the case of indecent exposure, common law considered it a public nuisance for anyone to publicly expose the naked person.

That sounds quite simple, except that, to be guilty, the offender had to *publicly* expose the naked person. There was nothing here about females being insulted or any wilful and lewd behaviour being a necessary ingredient – all that was needed was public exposure of the naked person. So if a man flashed from an hotel window, or the bedroom window of his own private house, was that illegal under common law? Common law reckoned that if it could be seen from a public place, or by the public in general, then it was illegal. That simplified things. Almost.

During my time at Aidensfield, I experienced two examples of a minor quandary involving that very point. Both happened at the same place. In the first instance, I was the person who saw two delightful young women who were completely naked as they frolicked in a small lake. The lake, around the size of three football pitches, belonged to Elsinby Estate and it was within the spacious grounds of the big house.

I had earlier received information from the estate manager that poachers were targeting the estate for pheasants; consequently I visited the grounds on regular occasions, both late at night and in the early hours of the morning, always on the look-out for suspicious vehicles or other indications that trespassers were present in the pursuit of game. Obviously, I did not use the open roads or the estate lanes and paths during those observations; because I had to be as secretive as possible, I moved stealthily through the trees and shrubs, making good use of the available cover, doing my best to become silent and invisible.

During one of those occasions, I was patrolling the park-land on a warm summer morning, poachers not caring for matters like closed seasons or whether their target birds had chicks. It would have been around 6.30 and the sun had risen some hours earlier to warm the air and bathe the countryside in its bright clear morning light. The landscape was rich with new blossom and their mingling scents, the birds were singing and nature was at its best. Even though I was working and clad in my uniform, the experience was wonderful, more so because I was making my way, as quietly as possible through dense woodland on the edge of the estate. Indeed my progress was very silent; the fallen leaves of autumn had long been absorbed by the ground or covered with new undergrowth and I could walk stealthily and virtually unseen as I made my way through the heavily leaved trees, shrubs and under-growth.

And then I heard a ripple of laughter. It was at a distance, somewhere beyond my vision but close enough for the sound to reach me. I stopped, all senses alert as I strained my ears in the hope I would hear it again. Poachers? As I stood motionless in absolute silence, there was not a sound other than a wren singing somewhere nearby. I was about to continue my route, thinking I'd been imagining things, when I heard it again. There was more laughter, but it was definitely a female voice. It was not far away either. At half past six in the morning? I wondered if it might be a female poacher accompanied by someone else, so I decided to try and find the source of that laughter. My keen sense of hearing had provided me with the general direction of the noise and so I began to creep through the trees, making as little sound as possible, as I edged my way towards the origin of the laughter.

It was repeated several times, with me drawing a little closer on each occasion. By this stage, I had decided there were two women. Each bout of laughter definitely sounded like two people. But I now found my route was taking me down a slight slope and on to a private estate road which took me beyond the cover of the trees. At the far side of the road was a slight rise in the ground with the slope being covered with dense rhododendron bushes, all higher than me. The bushes ran along the roadside for the full length of the lake, excellent cover, I thought; a very effective screen. Because I was on the road and momentarily beyond any kind of concealment, I hurried across and began to scramble up the slope and through the rhododendrons, still making very little noise. I could hear the laughter quite clearly now and when I crested the slope, without emerging from the rhododendrons, I could see the estate's beautiful lake.

And there were two completely naked young women, frolicking in the shallow water, splashing each other and then diving in for a brief swim before resuming more splashing. It was like a beautiful scene from one of the Greek legends with goddesses playing and laughing in the sunshine and I admit I remained hidden for a few minutes to enjoy the spectacle. The girls would be either in their late teens or early twenties, one very blonde and the other dark-haired, but each with the slender figure of youth and totally relaxed as they swam and played.

The big house was out of sight from my vantage point but I knew it was not far away across the lawns. Then, quite suddenly, they stopped their playing and ran to the shore, giggling and laughing as they made for the boathouse.

They disappeared inside to emerge a few minutes later wearing heavy dressing-gowns made from towelling, and then trotted across the lawns towards the big house. I realized they were guests, not trespassers or poachers, and when they were out of sight, it was time for me to leave. I made my way back into the woodland to continue my hunt for poachers but found no sign of any. I did not tell anyone about my wonderful experience for I did not want unwelcome people to venture down that lane in the hope of witnessing something similar. I was to learn later that there was a big family event in the Hall at that time, and no doubt those girls were guests.

It never crossed my mind that the girls might be committing an offence at common law – indeed, their behaviour was totally in private – but only a day later, a lady knocked at the door of my police house on the hilltop at Aidensfield. Her name was Miss Garrett and she lived behind the church at Elsinby.

Everyone in the village referred to her as Miss Garrett and I wondered if she had a first name. She had driven across to Aidensfield in her new Austin Mini, and when I opened the door I could see her Pekinese dog on the front seat, yapping at the window.

'Ah, Miss Garrett!' I welcomed her. 'Do come in.'

'I shall not stay longer than necessary, Constable,' She had a high-pitched voice which reminded me of a school ma'am who considered herself superior to the children. 'We can talk here, it won't take more than a minute. I have a complaint to make.'

'Well, please tell me and I'll deal with it.'

'Now, Constable, I am not an old fuddy-duddy but there are limits as to how one should behave in public, which is why I am here. I wish to complain about two naked women in Elsinby lake. Their behaviour was an affront to common decency.'

'Ah,' I said, realizing she must have seen what I had enjoyed only the previous day. 'You mean the lake on Elsinby estate?'

'What other lake would I mean in Elsinby, Constable?'

'It's just that it's on private property,' I countered. 'The relevant laws that deal with indecent exposure all refer to public places or streets. The lake is on private land, so where were you when you saw the women?'

'I was walking past, constable, early this morning. With Pinkie.'

'Pinkie?'

'My dog. I walk her along that road that passes through the estate and skirts the lake. It is one of my regular routes.'

'It's a private road,' I pointed out. 'I know the estate allows local people to walk along it or take their dogs, but it is not a public road, not for general use by all and sundry. The general public doesn't have access to the lake.'

'Constable, I have registered my complaint and I expect you to do something about it. There are certain standards which should be maintained, and parading naked in full view of members of the public is not something I can condone. If you will not do something about it, I shall write to the chief constable.'

'I will certainly look into the matter; I am merely trying to establish the facts.'

'The fact is that two young women were behaving in a shocking and indecent manner. What other fact is there?' And she stalked back to her car with all the majesty of a 65-year-old spinster as Pinkie yapped with delight at her return. All I could do now was check my law reference books.

Clearly, the Vagrancy Act did not apply because they were women and its relevant clause referred to men. The Town Police Clauses Act could not be invoked because it was effective only in certain urban areas. That left common law. For there to be an offence at common law, it was necessary that the naked person was *publicly* exposed. In simple terms, that meant it must be seen by members of the general public – someone in the privacy of his own house, for example, flashing to people in the street would be guilty. Common law demanded no intent to insult anyone or to cause annoyance – the mere act of publicly showing the naked person was sufficient. I was never sure whether this meant the entire body or only the very personal bits.

In thinking this through, my immediate opinion was that the girls had not committed any offence because the lake was on private property and their activities could not be seen by the general public. The lane was not open to everyone, it was available to the local people by consent of the estate. Indeed, only a few made use of it. Furthermore, the bank of rhododendrons provided a very solid screen and the lake could not be viewed through them; the only way for anyone to see the lake from there was to climb through the bushes. I guessed Miss Garrett must have done so, probably in pursuit of her dog.

Then I discovered a nineteenth-century case which referred to men bathing without any screen or covering so close to a public footpath that it was inevitable exposure of their 'persons' would occur; in that case, they were found guilty. Another case referred to a man who had persuaded some little girls to accompany him to a private place off a public footpath so that they were all out of sight from the path and there he exposed himself to them. In its infinite wisdom, the court decided that the man had no legal right to visit that place because it was private, but it accepted evidence that lots of people did visit that very place, all without permission, and so the man's act might have been witnessed by the public. He was convicted. But perhaps the real case for me to quote to Miss Garrett was one in which the court decided that even if the exposure was in a place of public resort but visible to only one person, then no offence was committed. A solitary person on his or her own was not considered to be *the public*.

Rather than visit Miss Garrett to say I could not take the matter any further, I decided to inform Sergeant Craddock and after due discussion, with him also checking in his law library, we decided we could not take any action. When I called, I think Miss Garrett expected me to announce I had arrested the two young women, but instead I had to say we would not be taking any further action. She was clearly very angry and said she would write to the chief constable, but I advised her against it, giving the relevant case law as my reason.

'Miss Garrett,' I said, as sternly as I could in the circumstances, 'I have visited the scene and I know that the lake is screened from the road by a dense hedge of rhododendron bushes. The only way you can see the lake is to climb through those bushes and if you did that, you might find yourself being prosecuted as a peeper, especially as that is private property.'

She glared at me, realizing I had found her weak spot.

At that moment, I knew she had been peeping! I rubbed it in. 'If those ladies had seen you and then complained about your conduct, you could find yourself being bound over to be of good behaviour by Ashfordly magistrates. I don't think you would want that.'

'It's a disgrace, Constable. I don't know what the world is coming to,' she said and she slammed the door.

I made sure her complaint was recorded in our Occurrence Book and that my action was included to explain and justify the outcome. We never heard from the chief constable so I can only presume she did not write to him, neither did we receive any more complaints from Miss Garrett.

And for the record, I never discovered the identity of those two bathing beauties.

I returned to the scene of the crime on several occasions – all in the furtherance of my duty of course – but found no further evidence of naked persons being exposed either in private or public.

Chapter 4

Claude Jeremiah Greengrass had an unsettling capacity for constantly appearing to get things wrong so far as the law was concerned. Because of this, he was in frequent conflict with the police although it was often found he was actually operating just within the limits imposed by Britain's statutes. He seemed to know precisely where the borderlines were drawn and it pleased him to operate on the very fringes of legality. Sometimes I felt he deliberately pushed the extent of his activities to the point of looking illegal even if they weren't just to see how the constabulary would respond. He loved to prove the police were wrong which is why he liked to bait and taunt the constabulary from time to time.

That kind of roguish red-rag-waving-at-a-bull began, I think, when Sergeant Blaketon repeatedly tried to book him for various misdemeanours, usually with little success. Their mutual antagonism persisted into Blaketon's retirement, but then Claude turned his attention towards newer members of the force. That he loved to taunt police officers was never in doubt and his behaviour was in the same vein as little lads who steal apples from the orchards of cantankerous old men while letting themselves be seen running away with two fingers in the air. Claude could also be likened to children who deliberately splash haughty adults with water from muddy puddles – it was mischief bordering on criminality.

Perhaps I should have sensed that something was afoot within the Greengrass camp when he stopped me in Aidensfield and asked, 'Ah, Constable Rhea, just the fellow. I'd like you to advise me on a matter of law.'

'Do you want to infringe a law, or find one you can't break?' I asked, tongue in cheek.

'Neither, I want to know if one exists for my particular set of circumstances.' His cunning old eyes glinted and blinked as he began to test me.

'All right, try me,' I said wondering what was coming next.

'Are there any rules about the colour of motor cars?' he put to me.

'How do you mean, rules about their colour?'

'Well,' and he continued to blink his rheumy old eyes at me. 'I mean, is there any colour I can't have on my car? Are some colours banned?'

'Well, Henry Ford once famously said you could have any colour of car you wanted, so long as it was black.'

'It's not black I want. You can get cars in all sorts of colours these days and I rather fancy a very bright one, Constable Rhea, one that'll stand out in a crowd or be prominent in a car-park. And I can tell you this, I'm not thinking of a Ford; I want something more exotic, something that will enhance my reputation and reveal my true character while being an asset to my business.'

'What on earth have you been reading?' I asked.

'I'm a businessman, in case you hadn't noticed, and we entrepreneurs have to be aware of the image we present to our customers and potential customers. So I thought a distinctive car in a distinctive colour would be a good idea. It will help me and my enterprises to get better known and that will increase my earning power and turnover.'

'You want to get noticed?'

'Aye, that's about it. I want people to see my car and recognize it immediately, so they'll come rushing to buy the top quality things I sell. I don't want to get lost in the crowd, you see, so if I go and park in the middle of Middlesbrough or Scarborough, or even somewhere down south like York, I want folks to say, "That must be Mr Greengrass". And with me being a law-abiding sort of chap, I don't want my car to break the law, you see, which is why I'm asking about colours.'

'Why do I suspect there is some kind of

hidden plot behind your apparently simple question?'

'That's just your highly suspicious policeman's mind, Constable. All I'm asking is if there's any colour I can't have. What about these psychedelic colours that are all the rage?'

'Isn't that what people see when they've been taking drugs?' I grinned.

'No, you daft bat! It's very bright colours, all swirling and distorted...'

'Like somebody mixing several tins of bright paint and throwing the result over a canvas to claim it's a work of art?'

'I'm getting nowhere fast here, I can see. So let's cut the cackle, shall we, and you tell me whether there's any law to prevent me having nice colours on my car.'

'No, Claude, there isn't such a law. The Construction and Use Regulations of 1963 lay down all sorts of rules and regulations about motor vehicles when they are on the road, but colour isn't one of the things which has attracted the legislators' attention. In other words, Claude, you can have any colour you want.'

'Or combination of colours?'

'Or combination of colours,' I agreed.

'Then that's all I want to know,' and he

turned to amble away chuckling to himself as I wondered what sort of motor monstrosity he was going to produce.

'Before you leave, Claude,' I called, to halt his departure, 'there's one thing to remember if you change the colour of your car.'

'Oh, aye, and what's that?'

'Any change has to be recorded in your car's registration book, and you must send the book to the registration authority for them to amend their records. That makes it all legal.'

'So what if it was originally made in bright colours? In a foreign country?'

'So long as all the details in the registration book are accurate, there's no problem.'

His eye-catching new purchase was revealed when the vehicle in question appeared in the village about three weeks later. Claude pulled up in front of the garage to fill the tank of his new dream machine and I happened to be there, topping up the police Mini-van with fuel. I had just gone inside to sign the chit for my petrol when the apparition appeared at the pumps. From inside, I thought it looked like a cross between a fairground spaceship and a child's drawing of Hell. At first, I had no idea this was Claude's new car; I thought it was a pop group who'd found the vehicle because it was a huge gaudy chromium-plated American model of the worst kind. I wasn't sure of the make or model, not without making a very close inspection.

When I ventured outside, dazzled by the apparition, I saw it was very wide and very long; in fact, it looked about as long and as wide as a fifty-seater bus. The bonnet was oblong and seemed to reach into eternity – in my view it looked big enough to contain my Mini-van, while I felt the boot could accommodate a double bed or even two singles side by side. The car was open-topped with massive black leather seats, and I could see a hood was present, but folded down. But the colour was the worst. It shrieked at everyone. There was not just one colour but hundreds on a background of what looked like a cross between salmon pink and orange. The entire body was covered with whirls and rings and long lines and squares and circles of every imaginable colour and shade. There was a fair amount of black, I noticed, just as if a child had walked along the car with a can of black paint and a brush in his hands. I was puzzled by the white rings which seemed to be spread haphazardly around the bodywork, like discarded halos. The walls of the tyres were painted white too.

Really, it was dreadful. It looked like a child's painting, but much bigger and infinitely worse. As I signed for my petrol, a small crowd began to gather around Claude's customized Cadillac, for that is what it was. He walked around it, flushed with pride and joy while explaining its secrets and gimmicks. He had wanted to attract attention and his plan appeared to be working. I must admit I did not know whether to laugh or cry.

'So what do you reckon, Constable? How's that for style and colour?'

'I'm speechless, Claude,' I had to admit. 'But you wanted your car to attract a crowd, and so you have.'

'This car will be my road to a fortune,' he said. 'The name of Greengrass will become known across the north as a by word for style and quality.'

'Well, all I can say is that I hope your plan is a success, but you realize that wherever you go in this, you'll attract attention.'

'That's just what I want, Constable, that's the whole idea. And if I attract the attention of the motor-patrolling constabulary, then I want everything to be legal and above board, don't I? It'll be properly taxed and insured; there'll be no dodgy tyres or duff exhaust pipes to land me in court, and I've made sure the registration book is up-to-date with these colours as you suggested. I'll set the best example of good roadsmanship ever seen in Aidensfield.'

'What a speech, Claude! Wonderful. You've become all legitimate! So what can I say, except the best of luck and *bon voyage?*'

Because I had an appointment in Elsinby, I left Claude to his admirers and wondered how this ghastly creation would be accepted in the calm countryside around Aidensfield. In the days and weeks which followed, Claude's distinctive car could be seen around the district, sometimes attending cattle markets or house sales, sometimes parked prominently in Ashfordly or one of the other nearby towns and often outside inns in the villages around the moors. Whenever it was parked at an isolated farmstead or lonely cottage, its presence was like a bright beacon against the dark backdrop of the moorland. Quite literally, it stuck out like a sore thumb. Even from a distance of several miles when viewed from lofty vantage points, it could be seen in a variety of lonely places, something which might prove useful should I ever need to ascertain the old rogue's whereabouts at a particular time. Certainly, Claude's travels around the moors could scarcely be more noticeable. Most people, although believing Claude had gone somewhat over the top in purchasing the Cadillac, found the entire experience quite amusing, with some even asking for a ride in it; certainly, it was very comfortable with its soft leather seats and well-sprung suspension. I did not receive any complaints about its garishness or mere presence: the local people appeared to accept it. With one exception.

Oscar Blaketon, my former sergeant and now public-house owner, took me to one side when I paid an official visit to his Aidensfield Arms.

'You'll have to do something about that monstrosity of Greengrass's,' he muttered, in what was an almost conspiratorial manner.

'Like what?' I asked. 'He's not breaking any laws, it's taxed and insured; all its working parts are in good order, there are no dangerous bits hanging off–'

'That might be so, but he parks it right outside my front door where it can be seen by all and sundry who pass through the village, and it's attracting the wrong sort of people into my establishment.'

'Wrong sort of people?'

'Passers-by, tourists on their way some-where, young fools most of them, trouble-makers, mods and rockers, teddy boys, drug dealers I wouldn't be surprised... They all think it belongs to some pop group or other and they come inside to find them. They can't believe it belongs to that old rogue, and it's not as if they stay and spend money because the moment they find it's not a pop group's passion wagon, they leave. And some get quite nasty; you should hear the language when they think they've been conned. I can forecast the day when they'll smash the furniture or throw bottles about in their frustration, all because of Claude's colourful Cadillac. And apart from anything else, its bonnet and back-end are so long that the car sticks into the road when it's at my front door, and that must be causing an obstruction!'

'Oscar, you of all people know very well that most of that is nothing to do with the police. The obstruction might be a matter for me, if indeed it causes one, but who comes into your premises is entirely your business, not mine. And I can't ban Claude or his car for what other people might do in your pub, and neither can you. Even if some of us don't like his car, it's harmless and

101

anyway, the chances are he'll soon get sick of it. It's like a new toy just now.'

'There must be something you can do, Nick. I'll bet it's not entirely legal; there'll be some American part which is not legal in this country, or some measurement that is too large or too small for English roads, or maybe the horn doesn't comply with our regulations, or the speed of flashing for its winking indicators ... if you were a traffic policeman who was an expert at his job, I bet you could find something wrong with it.'

'That would be police persecution, Oscar, and you know it. I can't go around checking things like that just because you don't like Claude!'

'I realize that, but what I'm saying is that if the law is being broken, you should do something about it.'

'It's not being broken, Oscar. I've had a good look around that car, and so far as I can see, everything's legal.'

'Well, I'll tell you what, if I was still your sergeant, I'd be ordering you to take that thing into a garage and go through it with a fine toothcomb; you'd be bound to find something dodgy that would be worth a summons.'

'That's not my style, Oscar, but if you get

real trouble in the bar from rowdy customers, let me know.'

'It might be too late by the time you lot
arrive! But remember what I've just said,
there must be something illegal about that
car!'

'I'll bear it in mind, Oscar.'

I was aware of the long-term enmity
between Blaketon and Greengrass but had
no wish to take sides; Oscar Blaketon was no
longer my sergeant and he must not be
allowed to dictate to me about my methods
of working. So far as I was concerned,
Claude was not committing any type of
traffic offence or nuisance with his car, and
when I checked to see if it was protruding
into the road to cause an obstruction outside
the pub, I saw it wasn't. It was well within the
sightline provided by the car-park wall, and I
would bear that in mind in case Blaketon
mentioned it again.

Over the next few weeks there was an un-
easy truce between Blaketon and me, with
him clearly refusing to mention Claude's
vehicle and me deciding not to mention it
unless Blaketon resurrected the matter. But
he was constantly riled by the mere thought
of its presence, even if he could do nothing
about it, and when it parked outside his

front door, it was guaranteed that he would become grumpy and bad-tempered, usually popping out to see if it was causing an obstruction.

Then, one Wednesday lunchtime, half-a-dozen noisy youths surged into the bar of the Aidensfield Arms. At the time, Claude's car happened to be parked at the front and I was in the bar, off duty, having a quiet drink with a colleague from Thirsk, a detective called Colin. He had been passing through Aidensfield and had popped in on the off-chance of catching me for a chat over a pint and a sandwich apiece.

The boisterous new arrivals were dressed in jeans and black leather jackets, and their hair was uniformly long and greased; they were brash and confident, laughing and joking as they spoke in loud voices while making for the bar to order sandwiches and pints. Blaketon, no doubt with half a mind not to serve them, could not find a legitimate reason for declining their custom, so he pulled the pints and called to Gina to produce the necessary sandwiches. At least he had the courtesy not to draw attention to me and Colin, but I guessed he was pleased we were there.

As the loud group settled down with their

meal at a table in a corner, one of them finished early and came across to ask Blaketon, in a surprisingly polite and well-spoken manner, 'Excuse me, but can you tell me who owns the car outside? The Cadillac.'

'It's a local second-hand dealer,' grunted Blaketon. 'Name of Greengrass; he's in the snug just now, playing dominoes.'

'Nice set of wheels, man.' Another of the lads had come to the bar, having finished his meal. 'Very nice set of wheels.'

'If you like that sort of thing!' Blaketon had no idea how to respond.

'We love that sort of thing, man,' the second one said. 'Do you think he would sell it?'

'I doubt it, he hasn't owned it for long but you can ask him. I'll call him through.' And then he shouted, 'Claude, you've a fan interested in that car of yours.'

Moments later, Claude came into the bar, followed by Alfred his dog. He blinked at the crowd of youths, then looked at me and my friend before asking, 'Well, who wants to know what? Claude Jeremiah Greengrass at your service.'

It was the well-spoken lad who responded. 'We like your car, Mr Greengrass, we had a good look at it before we came in. Nice machine. What will you take for it?'

'Take for it? It's not for sale, I've not had it very long; I'm just getting used to it.'

'What did you pay for it?'

'That's between me and my piggy bank,' grinned Claude.

'Well, as you know, a top-of-the-range English car, in new condition, is about a thousand pounds, or up to fifteen hundred in some cases. Good family saloons are about seven or eight hundred when they're new.'

'Aye, but mine's not new. I got it second-hand, or something like that. From a friend of a friend.'

'But it's a nice one. I can see it's not new, but knowing what prices these American vehicles fetch in England, I'd say you paid about five hundred at the most for this one, perhaps less. Even down to three-fifty.'

'So what are you getting at?' asked Claude.

'I'd like to buy your car, Mr Greengrass.'

'I've told you, it's not for sale.'

'But you might be persuaded, if the price was right.'

'If you knew how long it took me to find this one, which is just what I want for my expansive future business plans, you'd know I would never sell it, no matter how much you offer,' said Claude, not very convincingly.

'Twelve hundred pounds, Mr Greengrass. Cash. In notes. No cheques.'

Claude spluttered in his surprise. 'Twelve hundred pounds? You mean one thousand two hundred pounds? In notes?'

'That's what I said. Think about it, Mr Greengrass. We'll return a week today, to give you time to think about it.'

'But ... but ... I mean ... why would you want this car?'

'I'm the manager of a pop group, Mr Greengrass; we've just made a new single and it's climbing the charts as I speak ... it'll be number one before the month's out, you'll see. That's these lads here, they're the Heartbeats. We're on our way to the top, Mr Greengrass. Now, though, we're off to Redcar, Whitby, Scarborough and Bridlington doing gigs we booked earlier, but we want something better than the beat up old van we're using, something befitting the style of our modern music. That car of yours is perfect! We'll keep the van for our instruments and the car for showing the lads off to their fans.'

'Aye, well, I mean...'

'Don't make your decision now. Think about it until next Wednesday, then we'll be back here for more sandwiches. If you do sell it, though, we'll want to take it there and then, with all its documents in order, ready for the road. My name is Mike Redland, I'm the manager of the Heartbeats. Remember the name, Mr Greengrass! Heartbeats.'

'Aye, well, this is all a bit sudden...'

'That's why you've got a week to make up your mind. See you in here next Wednesday. If you have the car ready, I'll have the cash. Come on, lads, we can't hang about here, we've a rehearsal to get through before tonight's gig.'

And as quickly as they had arrived, they departed. Quite suddenly, the bar went very quiet with its few customers watching Claude to see how he would react. The offer had certainly not been very private and Claude stared at them as they left, watching them through the window as they examined his car before roaring away in their battered old van.

'What do think about that?' he asked those of us who were in the bar.

'Conmen, Claude, out to get your car with a load of fake notes, I'll bet,' said Blaketon.

'I don't think so.' My pal Colin now entered the fray. 'I've heard their music, the Heartbeats. He's right, they are going places. That new single is racing up the charts ... 'Lovebeat' it's called. Very romantic, very modern though. If I was you, Mr Greengrass, I'd be here next Wednesday with all your car's paperwork ready for a quick sale.'

'I don't know what to say,' and, unaccountably lost for words, Claude and Alfred went outside. We watched through the bar windows as he stood and looked at his pride and joy, stroking its paintwork and walking around it as if in a daze.

'He won't be able to refuse that sort of money, especially when it's in cash,' said Blaketon. 'If it's real, that is.'

'And even if they are undesirable types attracted into your pub by his car!' I couldn't resist that retort. 'If I were you, Oscar, I'd pass word around that the Heartbeats are coming to the Aidensfield Arms next week – you might get a full house, and even an impromptu concert or rendition of 'Lovebeat' ... the Heartbeats could put Aidensfield on the map, thanks to Claude!'

'All right, Nick, don't rub it in! Let's all wait to see what next Wednesday brings, eh? And I wonder if anyone from around here is going to any of those gigs?'

'I'd like to go.' Gina had reappeared from the kitchen. 'Mebbe they need a girl vocalist, eh? I thought they were real nice guys and I'll bet the Heartbeats become a real success. Fancy them coming in here though – and fancy coming back!'

'Don't get worked up about it all,' cautioned Blaketon. 'Things might not work out. You might never see them again.'

Word soon spread around Aidensfield and district that the Heartbeats had promised to visit the pub the following Wednesday lunchtime, and the interest increased due to the well-publicized success of their single, currently number three in the charts. Even though it was a Wednesday with most of the young people at work, some had managed to get time off. I was on duty but I could pay an official visit to the Aidensfield Arms, just to ensure there was no trouble. When I arrived soon after twelve, the place was packed, the car-park was full and cars were even parked along the street. But Blaketon had cheered everyone by placing a large 'Reserved for Mr Greengrass' sign outside the pub's front door, beside another reserved for the Heartbeats.

'I've got sandwiches ready for them,' Blaketon told me. 'I've reserved the snug so they can have their meal in peace, on the house too; the rest of the customers will have to pack themselves into the bar and dining-room. So what has Claude decided about his car? Any idea?'

'No idea,' I had to admit. 'I've seen him around the village over the past few days, but he's been keeping very quiet about it all. What I have noticed, though, is that his car is as clean as a new pin, much cleaner than he usually keeps it. That makes me think he'll sell it and put the money towards something equally bizarre.'

'Well, we'll just have to wait and see. I just hope those lads turn up as they promised. You don't think they were kidding Greengrass, do you? Playing some kind of trick on him?'

'Who knows?'

We received our answer at quarter to one. Heartbeats fans had gone outside with their drinks to await the arrival of their heroes and when the battered old van appeared outside Aidensfield Stores, a mighty cheer arose when someone sighted it. What had originally been little more than a car-buying exercise had now become something of a major public event and the group was cheered through the village as they headed for the pub. I was outside in my uniform and waved to attract the driver's attention, directing him to the reserved parking space and so Aidensfield became the venue of hundreds of Heartbeats fans. We ushered the lads inside, but it was far from easy, getting them through the crush and into the snug, but in time, we succeeded. A few minutes later, Blaketon rang the bell on the bar, the one usually sounded to signify the end of drinking-up time, and called for silence.

'Ladies and gentlemen, thank you for turning out to give such a warm welcome to the Heartbeats. Mike Redland, their manager, has asked if they can have a few minutes to themselves while having lunch, and during that time they have a small business matter to attend to. Then they must leave us very soon afterwards because they have commitments later today in Liverpool. However, they are prepared to spend half an hour singing for us but there is not enough room in here. I have the key to the village hall, and the caretaker's permission to use it – but the floor needs to be cleared of chairs and card tables after last night's whist drive and the stage has to be prepared. Can I ask for volunteers to do that? You have about twenty minutes to get things ready...'

The pub emptied rapidly as an army of volunteers raced up the village to prepare the hall and I must admit I was impressed by Blaketon's handling of the event; clearly, he had made earlier plans because he wanted everything to be successful. I went along to the hall to make sure the group's van could find a parking space close to the rear entrance because they would need to unload their equipment.

Not many minutes later, with the hall's floor cleared and the stage ready, I saw Claude's colourful Cadillac cruising up the village with the group's old van behind it. Claude was driving the Cadillac with the Heartbeats waving at the crowds from the open-topped vehicle, and their manager was following in the van. At that stage, I had no idea whether Claude had sold his car but it didn't matter – he was truly enjoying his few minutes of fame. I didn't see Alfred during these events; I think he'd been left at home.

The Heartbeats provided free entertainment for half an hour, concluding with a rousing rendition of their hit single, 'Lovebeat' and then they had to leave. They left as they had arrived, with one of the group driving Claude's car. Clearly, he had decided to part with it. The manager followed in the battered old van. The group were cheered as they disappeared out of the village towards the distant moors. Claude was one of the people who stood and watched their departure and I swore I could see moistness in his eyes as his pride and joy vanished from sight.

'So you sold it, Claude,' was all I could think of saying.

'I couldn't refuse, could I?' he spoke quietly. 'Not an offer like that, and they promised me free tickets to their shows.'

Then Blaketon came to join us.

'Everything seemed to go very well.' He spoke to no one in particular. 'Nice lads, eh? A cut above your normal rowdy music makers.'

'They're heading for the top, I'm sure; they are musical, not just drummers and guitar strummers. They can actually sing in tune and play real music,' I said.

Then Blaketon surprised us all. 'Come on, Claude, I owe you a free drink,' he said.

'A free drink? Aye, I think you do,' chuckled Claude. 'Make it a big one, then I'll raise my glass to the Heartbeats.'

With the profit Claude received from the sale of his car, plus an injection from some of his hoarded cash, he bought a brand new Morris Commercial truck, the first new vehicle he had ever owned. He was immensely proud of it. It was a rich dark-maroon colour with smart black mudguards and a rear space which could carry everything from livestock to large items of furniture. The cab was large enough to seat three men side by side, certainly ideal for transporting Alfred, his scruffy dog. Far more soberly adorned than his Cadillac, it was a very wise purchase and would be ideally suited for his business as a general dealer and, with such a capacity, he could even carry loads for other people, provided he obtained the correct Carrier's Licence. I think he quite fancied himself as a haulier and he even went to see a signwriter who painted the cab doors with the words 'Claude Jeremiah Greengrass, Hagg Bottom, Aidensfield' and his telephone number.

In a very short time, Claude's new truck was just as familiar a sight around Aidensfield and Ashfordly as his Cadillac had been, and it could be seen attending farm sales, livestock marts, the sales of house and office contents, plant sales and almost any place where Claude felt he might make a useful profit by buying something and later selling it. The fact he held a 'C' Carriers' Licence meant he could not transport, for hire or reward, the goods of other people; for that he would need either an 'A' or 'B' licence both of which were more difficult to obtain. Whether Claude could carry the goods of other people without charging them was another matter and, knowing Claude as I did, it would not surprise me if he 'helped' or 'did favours' for his friends and contacts without any apparent charge. Even if he accepted goods in lieu of payment, that would amount to 'reward' and thus be illegal, and although the police may be unable to catch Claude operating such a scheme, it was a racing certainty that other properly licensed carriers would quickly make a fuss. They would not want Greengrass taking business away from them.

The outcome of Claude's new enthusiasm with his truck was that wherever Claude went, the truck was sure to be there. He even drove it to the pub when he popped in for a drink or two; he drove it to the surgery when he went to collect some medicine, and even parked it outside church when he was guest at a wedding. It was obvious to the village that Claude and his new truck were inseparable and this pleased them because they knew it had been such a wrench to part with his Cadillac, even though the method of its departure had been so pleasurable and memorable. And then someone stole it.

Leaving Alfred at home, he had driven to a saleroom in Ashfordly to collect a sideboard he had bought, ostensibly to furnish his own dining-room. With helpers from the auctioneer's office, the sideboard had been loaded into the rear of Claude's truck, but before returning to Aidensfield he had to visit the bank. Although most of his dealings were in cash and therefore unrecorded, he did maintain a bank account mainly for appearances, just in case the Income Tax authorities came along to inspect his books. He drove to the bank that morning shortly after it opened, parked outside and went in to complete a transaction, paying in some cash and withdrawing more for his petty-cash account. There was a small queue and so his business took longer than expected.

When he emerged, his truck had vanished together with the sideboard. His reaction was one of utter disbelief. He thought someone must have moved it a little further along the street, perhaps to let a bus get past, and for the first few minutes he ran up and down seeking his truck. But it had vanished completely. By chance, I was in Ashfordly Police Station when he rushed in to report it.

'It happened in minutes!' His voice revealed his distress. 'I just went into the bank and when I came out, it had gone. You'll have to get it back, Constable, it's my livelihood, I can't work without it.'

'I hope it's not damaged.' I took particulars including its make, model, colour and registration number, not forgetting the sideboard. 'I'll circulate it immediately, Claude, to our traffic cars and foot patrols. If it's only just been taken it'll probably be on the road somewhere nearby, our lads will check all roads out of Ashfordly.'

'What can I do?'

'Tell as many people as you can, friends, colleagues, people you know who live hereabouts, ask them to keep an eye open for it, but not necessarily on the road. It might have been taken by a joy-rider and dumped in a wood or on the moors, or taken to some other town. How much petrol was there in the tank?'

'Enough for twenty-five or thirty miles, I'd say.'

'Enough to get well clear of Ashfordly. So how did they manage to steal it so quickly? You didn't leave the keys in the ignition, did you?'

'Aye, I did, and now I know I shouldn't have, but I was only going in the bank for a minute or two... I mean, you don't expect folks to pinch your truck, do you?'

'Thieves have no respect for other people, Claude; they're among the most selfish of people. Now, hang on if you like, while I radio this to all our stations, our mobiles and all our foot patrols, not just here in Ashfordly and district, but throughout the county and beyond, then you can see just what we'll do for you.'

I wanted him to see that we took such matters very seriously and did our best to recover any stolen property. Early reports were always beneficial because it reduced the time during which a thief could dispose of his ill-gotten gains, and in the case of a motor vehicle, a swift response often led to a rapid recovery. Claude listened as I gave details to our force control room and to Divisional Headquarters, asking that all roads leading from Ashfordly be checked because the truck had only vanished within the last fifteen minutes or so. Claude was as happy as he could be under the circumstances.

He understood I could not give chase because I had no idea which road the stolen truck had taken; besides, I had to remain in the office to take charge of the search. Claude said he would go into town and visit all his mates in their pubs and business premises to tell them about his loss, and ask that they keep their eyes open and get their customers and clients to do the same. I said I'd ring Blaketon and various people around Aidensfield to ask them to do likewise and then, if it was not recovered, I would contact the local newspaper to ask them to highlight the crime. However it was published only once a week on Fridays, and it was Tuesday now. Nonetheless, between us we would ensure that the police and public kept their eyes open for Claude's missing truck.

What was to later emerge was that the people of the district were still experiencing a warm glow of gratitude to Claude for his part in getting the Heartbeats to visit Aidensfield, and many of them were aware of the sacrifice he had made in parting with his beloved Cadillac. Those who learned of his loss through the proverbial bush tele-graph system which operates so successfully and swiftly in rural areas, immediately decided to positively hunt for Claude's truck. For example, instead of driving past, say, the entrance to quarry or wood, they would drive in to see if it had been aban-doned out of sight of the road. And so began a massive example of police and public co-operation, and all because Claude had had tears in his eyes when his Cadillac was driven away by that pop group. The fact he had made a handsome profit did not seem to enter the equation. I was quite touched by this show of sympathy for him.

The result was a happy one for Claude but not for a certain brewery representative. The representative, Michael Stewart, had been visiting the remote moorland inn called the Moorcock which was about twenty miles from Ashfordly and when he had concluded his business with the landlord, went out to find his car missing. Although it was during opening hours, there were no customers at the inn because it was not yet lunchtime, and so Mr Stewart's car had been the only one in the car-park. And when he had left, there was a maroon-coloured Morris Commercial truck parked almost where his car had been.

While Mr Stewart rang the police from the Moorcock, the landlord went outside to look at the lorry and immediately realized it belonged to Claude. Word had already reached him about Claude's loss and so, when the police came to examine it for fingerprints, I soon received a radio call from the Scenes of Crime team to tell me that Claude's lorry had been found undamaged and with the keys still in the ignition. Clearly, a joy-rider had been taking vehicles without their owners' consent. The trail of other abandoned cars suggested he had started in Hull, taking a convenient car and then abandoning it after a short time, probably so that he would not be caught in possession of it. He also abandoned them when their fuel tanks were dangerously low. The trail of stolen and abandoned cars eventually ended in Newcastle-on-Tyne, but the thief was never caught.

When eventually I managed to trace Claude and tell him the good news, he said it was his turn to buy drinks all round in the Aidensfield Arms. And so we had a lively party that night.

'I hope you've not left the keys in the ignition tonight!' I chided him.

'Oh God,' he said, and rushed out to retrieve them.

Chapter 5

If the weather is a constant topic of conversation among English people, then it is more so among those living in the wilds of the great British countryside. The reason for this is very simple – the work and mode of life of many country-folk can be seriously affected by the weather, either for good or bad. The weather is something which must be respected and considered on a daily basis. Even now, northern country dwellers will prepare for winter by stocking up on fuel, food and other essentials quite early during the autumn. In addition, they make sure they carry a shovel in their car from October through to March. If an inch of snow can disable southern suburbia and bring to a halt traffic in any Midlands town, it takes much more than that to immobilize a north-country dweller.

Equally importantly, country people must consider the welfare of their livestock, the productivity of farms and gardens, the ability to visit friends or relations or to go shopping for essentials, or even how to get to work. All this and more could, and still can, be frustrated by a severe bout of bad weather in the form of snow, gales, floods, frosts or even long periods of hot, dry sunshine. In spite of this, people would produce good crops of vegetables and fruit from their own gardens, eggs from their hens, bacon and ham from their pigs, plus fat and foods from their flocks of geese. Getting the best from those reserves of livestock and garden produce meant it was very important to plan ahead – seeds had to be planted on particular dates, geese were expected to begin laying on a certain day and crops had to ripen at the most advantageous time.

Country people, therefore, have become very adept at preparing for whatever form of weather nature chooses to hurl at them. Many of their anticipatory skills come from an instinct inherited from their forebears but now, thanks to efficient long-range weather-forecasting systems, much of that bygone uncertainty has been removed.

In spite of modern forecasting techniques, however, lots of rural householders continue to rely on well-known weather lore, even though the English calendar was changed in 1792 to render some sayings rather valueless. Even in Protestant England, saints' days continued to be very important in the rural calendar but so was the observation of weather patterns which affected local features like lakes, rivers and mountains.

Red sky at night, shepherd's delight is very well known all over most of England as a means of forecasting that a fine day will follow that colourful sky, and *red sky in the morning, shepherd's warning* means that a bad day is approaching. Something like *When Roseberry Topping wears a cap, Cleveland may beware a clap* is infinitely more local but probably just as important. Roseberry Topping is a prominent hill on the edge of the Cleveland Hills which in turn are part of the North York Moors, and that saying is thought to warn the locals that if the hilltop is shrouded in mist or cloud, then thunder or storms may follow.

The behaviour of animals, birds, insects and even flowers also provided information from which the weather might be forecast. It is said, for example, that if ladybirds hibernate in high places such as behind the bark of trees or inside window frames, then a mild winter can be expected, but if they hibernate at ground level, under leaves or clumps of grass, then we can expect a severe winter with frost and snow. A lot of berries on trees like the holly, rowan or hawthorn are also said to forecast a bad winter, this being nature's way of providing food for the birds during the worst of the weather.

There are thousands of examples of this kind of lore and much of this bygone expertise and knowledge was passed from parent to child *ad infinitum,* and so, even in the 1960s, youngsters would often quote verses or dates which were important to the world of local weather forecasting. For example, many are still brought up to believe that *if Candlemas Day be fair and bright, winter will have another flight, but if Candlemas be heavy with rain, winter will not come again.* Candlemas Day, 2 February, is widely regarded as the halfway stage of winter and much faith was – and still is – placed in this old adage. At that point of the year, there are still more than six weeks of winter remaining during which very bad weather can occur. Snow is by no means restricted to Christmas and January!

During my constabulary duties around Aidensfield and district, I encountered many of these beliefs when old men would sagely warn me of some impending weather-borne doom.

For example, one Monday morning an old chap told me to be sure and carry a raincoat that day because the leaves of his poplar trees were turning over in the breeze to show their undersides. A sure sign of rain, he warned me. And he was right. It rained quite heavily before the day was over.

Perhaps the most reliable of weather-forecasting plants is the scarlet pimpernel, often called the poor man's weather-glass or the shepherd's sundial. The flowers open only for a short time each day, usually between 8 a.m. and 3 p.m., but they always close in dull weather and will do so just before it rains. A pimpernel flower which is closed during a fine day is a sure sign of impending rain, but this kind of forecast is very short-term. What the country dweller needs is something which can forecast the state of the weather some days, weeks or even months ahead. And that is never easy, even for professional forecasters.

The following are just a few examples of how country folk forecast the weather some distance ahead. They believe that a thin skin on an onion means a mild winter to follow, while a thick skin heralds a hard winter, or that a profusion of whitethorn blossom heralds a tough winter later in the year. *If the ash tree comes into leaf before an oak we can expect a soak,* i.e. heavy rain during the summer, *but if the oak is in leaf before the ash, then we may only have a splash,* ie a dry summer. When dandelions bloom later than normal, i.e. a dry summer is heralded and, of course, the old favourite was to hang a piece of seaweed in an outbuilding. If it remained dry, the weather would remain dry, but if it turned damp, then rain could be expected. Another old favourite method of forecasting was the state of one's rheumatics. If one's joints became more painful than usual, then rain could be anticipated, while some believed that a ringing in the ears heralded strong winds.

Cats are said to become unusually active and playful before a storm, or to indulge in lots of washing of their faces before it rains, whilst among the birds of this country, rooks are widely known as weather forecasters. Generally, they are said to herald rain if they tumble about in the sky, or fall suddenly as if they've been shot, or even when they stay at home in their rookeries instead of going out to forage for food. In some parts of Yorkshire, it is claimed that rooks will congregate on the dead branches of trees if rain is expected before nightfall, but if the weather is going to be fine during the day, they will stand on living branches. Rooks are not the same as crows, however. Crows are solitary birds, usually living alone or perhaps in pairs but rooks are sociable and live in huge colonies, nesting in large number in the tree tops. A rook can be identified at close quarters because the base of its beak is bald, said to be due to it digging for food. If there is just one or two, therefore, they'll be crows; if there is a flock, they will be rooks.

It is inevitable that people ask whether our birds, animals, insects and plants can really foretell the weather and predict other things, or whether such beliefs have no real foundation in reality. Certainly, when the infamous tsunami devastated countries around the Indian Ocean on Boxing Day, 2004, much of the wild life which lived near the coast had already fled to safety inland, doing so hours before the wave struck. Even some dogs had fled, and domesticated elephants had seen fit to break loose and hurry to the safety of high ground before the wave appeared. So how did they know?

I experienced an example of that kind of animal forecasting in Aidensfield but it involved rooks, not dogs or elephants. I was undertaking one of my regular foot patrols around Elsinby one spring morning when I noticed someone working on the foundations of a new house. The necessary hole had been excavated so that the footings and channels for the various services could be installed. At that moment, there was nothing on the site except a big hole which was being enlarged when I arrived. The site was on the lower slopes of a hillside with a heavily wooded area immediately behind, rich with mature deciduous trees. I knew the builder and so, naturally curious as to what was going to be erected and who would live there, I stopped for a chat. Finding out about such things was all part of my job; we called it acquiring local knowledge. Local knowledge is very important in good police work.

'Good morning, Jim,' I greeted him. 'Looks like a nice job you've got.'

'A new house for a chap moving out from Leeds,' he smiled. 'Big place with four bedrooms and a double garage. It's going to be built in local stone with every modern convenience and very up-to-date equipment inside. I should finish by late November; he wants to move in for Christmas.'

Jim Green then invited me to look around and provided a guided tour of the site, explaining where the garage would be, which would be the living-room with a nice view, where the internal staircase would be and so forth. Jim, who had only recently launched himself as a self-employed builder, was clearly very pleased to have won this commission.

As we chatted though, a local character who was walking his dog arrived and stared at the hole in the ground.

'A house is it, Jim?' The new arrival was a retired farmer called Joe Grantley.

'Aye, for a customer in Leeds,' said Jim.

'Well, if it was me, I wouldn't build it there.' Joe shook his head knowingly.

'It's his choice,' responded Jim. 'He bought the whole site, the wood and the field included, and this is where he wants his house to be. He's had an architect in to design it. He's the customer, Joe, he calls the tune.'

'Well, if it was me, I should advise him to put it further away from those trees. He's got plenty more space so that's not a problem.'

'He's had them examined by a forestry expert, they're mature trees but not old ones, they're all quite sound and out of the line of gales. The experts have said they're not likely to cause problems, not with their roots spreading into the foundations or with falling branches. The architect looked at them too and he reckons they'll not be a problem. If my client gets too worried about them, he can always have them felled.'

'If I was him, I'd have them felled before the house goes up, well, not all of them, but those closest to the house, those that might fall into the garden. If I was you, Jim,' he stressed pointedly, 'I'd mention it to the chap who's commissioned you to build it; send him a letter, make sure you put it in writing.'

'Put what in writing?'

'Tell him those trees just behind the house, on that hillside, could prove danger-ous in the future because they might fall down. Not just branches, I mean, but the whole tree. If just one of them did, it would fall into the garden and somebody might be there even if it didn't reach the house. I'd say he should either change his building site or fell them.'

'I told you, he's gone into all that, Joe; he's happy the house is not in danger.'

'Well, it's up to him. I'm not thinking of the house but folks who might be in that garden, walking dogs, enjoying the sunshine or whatever. But mark my words, those trees right behind where his house is going are likely to come down of their own accord, in a gale or just through disease or something. I think he should be told.'

'So how do you know, Joe, when all the experts say he's no need to worry?' Jim asked, clearly thinking it was none of the old fellow's business.

'The rooks aren't nesting there. See? They're in almost every other part of that wood, nests all over the place, but not in those few trees just behind the house. That means the rooks know that something's going to happen to those few trees or mebbe just one of 'em. Disease mebbe, storm damage or summat.'

'Rooks can't know that...'

'They can, my lad! You bet they can. I can tell stories of rooks not nesting in old elms which tumbled to earth in gales years later ... mark my words, Jim, those old birds aren't so daft. Well, I've done what I can, I've told you, and like I said, if you've any sense, you'd tell your friend to do summat now, before it's too late.'

And Joe stalked away with his dog. As he was departing, Jim turned to me. 'What do you reckon about that, Nick?'

'I've heard that tale about rooks, Jim. They say they don't build their nests in trees which might come down, even some years ahead, but I've never known whether to believe it or not. But I think Joe's right – it might be a good idea to tell your client in Leeds what you've heard, then you're covered if anything does go wrong. Felling them seems the simplest thing if he's committed to this particular part of the site, so I think a phone call or letter would be worth it. If I were you, I'd put it in writing, just to tell him what Joe's told you.'

'Well, we've got planning permission for the house to be built right here but there's nothing much happening at the moment except a big hole so it wouldn't be too expensive to move further away from those trees, just in case one of them did come down. It might be cheaper than having the trees felled, it's not the easiest of access to that wood. So thanks, yes, I'll drop him a line, it shouldn't delay things too much and I'd rather get things right.'

Following Jim's letter, the owner of the new house actually drove out from Leeds to have another look at the site. Later, Jim explained to me that his client loved woods and trees which was why he had wanted the house constructed at this precise location but after further consultation with his architect and the planning authorities, the site of the house was relocated fifty yards further away from the woodland. Once again, Jim began work in earnest.

The splendid stone house was completed on time.

At Christmas, the trees were bare, having shed their leaves in the autumn and at this stage, the garden of the new house was nothing but a distant dream. At that time, it resembled nothing more than a building site in a field, but within a few years, it would be a beautiful addition to the house. The newly installed owner, a Mr Charles Fisher, organized a house-warming party on Boxing Day as a means of meeting his new neighbours and thanking those who had contributed to his fine home, including me and Mary, Jim and Farmer Joe. He had a special word of thanks for Joe, even though none of the trees had tumbled. It seemed Mr Fisher had taken Joe's advice very seriously.

And then in the following March, the winds developed into powerful gusts, the month living up to its ancient Anglo-Saxon names of Hreth-monath or Hyldmonath, the stormy or windy month. The date was 19 March, the feast day of St Joseph who was husband of the Virgin Mary. There used to be an old saying in Yorkshire that *If St Joseph's be clear, so follows a fertile year* and it was also a good day on which to get married. In general, though, March is said to be the month of many weathers due to the variety of conditions which occur and it is widely said that *if March comes in like a lion, it will go out like a lamb,* and vice versa. In this case, the storms were in the middle of the month and when Mr Fisher looked out of his bathroom window one morning, he saw several trees lying on the ground. The gale-force winds had ripped along the edge of the wood behind his house – and so the rooks had been proved right. Most of the fallen trees were found to be diseased and those which had been brought down had crashed against others to demolish them.

From that point onwards, Jim's reputation as a thoughtful and reliable builder became almost legendary and customers flocked to him for their building requirements. Farmer Joe's forecasting abilities were definitely taken more seriously thereafter and even when taking short walks in the local woodlands, the people of Aidensfield, Elsinby and district always checked to see which trees were ignored by the local colony of rooks.

I was not surprised when Mr Fisher named

his new house Rookwood.

During my patrols, I came across similar tales on the moors and in the dales, one of which concerned a lush field beside the river at Crampton. It was owned by Sam Bradshaw, one of the first farmers I had encountered on being posted to Aidensfield. The field extended along the riverside for several hundred yards. At this point, the banks were fairly high and the river had never been known to flood the village, although there was often flooding along its lower reaches, several miles downstream. Due to the lush nature of the field, its large size and sheltered position, Sam used it for grazing by his herd of dairy Redpolls. They could often be seen here, contently chewing the cud in what was a relaxed and traditional rural scene of the very best kind, the stuff of rustic paintings and photographs.

One February day I was patrolling the streets of Crampton when a car eased to a halt at my side. It was a rather elderly green Ford Prefect, although in a clean and tidy condition. The driver switched off the engine and climbed out.

He was in his early fifties, I estimated, with a somewhat emaciated and rather stooped appearance. His hair was fair almost to the point of being grey and it was thinning at the temples.

'Ah, just the man,' he said, panting slightly. 'Are you the local policeman?'

'Yes; PC Rhea. I'm based at Aidensfield but this village, Crampton, is on my beat.'

'Good, then you might be able to help me. I'm interested in that field beside the river, just this side of the bridge.' He pointed in the general direction. 'The one with all those red cows in it.'

'Right, I know it, so how can I help?'

'Do you know who the owner is?'

'I do, it's a farmer called Sam Bradshaw; he lives at Low Mires Farm between here and the bridge. There's a name sign on the gate.'

'Thanks; now, what sort of a man is he?'

'How do you mean, what sort of a man?'

'Well, is he kindly, does he take to strangers, or is he awkward and cantankerous?'

'He's in his sixties, if that's any help, but so far as I know he's quite affable and tolerant to most people. Why do you ask?'

'I run a boy-scout troop in Leeds and I'm looking for a nice site for our summer camp. We like very rural locations because most of our lads aren't in the least familiar with the countryside, and if possible we like them to experience real life, like seeing cows milked, pigs fed, eggs collected from hens and so on. I want to ask him if we can use his field for our camp and whether he'll let the lads feed the animals or watch milking time. Even help to muck them out. That sort of thing.'

'Well, all you can do is ask,' I smiled, not wanting to say that old Sam was somewhat wary of strangers and townies in particular. He accepted me because I could speak to him in the local dialect and had once helped him to obtain permission to fish on the River Esk. But he was kindly and approachable. 'He's usually around the premises at this time of day; he has a daughter called Mary who looks after him and the house. She's a bit on the shy side.'

'Thanks, I'll go and talk to him. We need to come in July, when the weather is milder and the schools are on holiday, for a week if possible.'

'The only thing I can tell you is that he puts his dairy herd out to grass in that field, but he does rotate them into other fields to give the grass chance to replenish itself. So there you are – and the best of luck.'

'Is it all right if I leave my car here?'

'No problem,' I assured him, and off he went on his mission. I had an appointment in Ploatby and left Crampton before I discovered the outcome of that visit. A few weeks later I paid a return visit to Crampton and spotted Sam plodding along the street. He stopped at my side.

'Now then, Mr Rhea,' he said. 'Not a bad morning for the time of year.'

'Very middlin', Sam, very middlin',' I responded.

'I'm off to get some stamps at the post office, not that I'm any good at this letter-writing lark but there's that many forms to fill in these days. I don't know what happens to 'em but I suppose it all keeps some young lasses in work, shoving paper about. Costs me a fortune in stamps, it does.'

While he was chatting, I remembered the scout-master's visit, and thought I would ask what had transpired.

'Oh, aye, that chap called to see me,' he grinned. 'I said yes, he can fetch his lads because yon field'll be empty for a week or two in July. He reckons they'll help me feed up and muck out and there'll be dads and older brothers with the lads as well, helping out. Besides, Mr Rhea, I reckon townies should know more about the countryside and if I can do owt to help 'em learn, then I will. And it's best if they start young.'

'Nice to hear it, Sam. Well done. I'm sure they'll enjoy the experience.'

That kind of development was of no real concern to me, although it was wise to be aware of the presence of a crowd of youngsters in a village, just in case something went awry. But I didn't expect Sam to ring me in something of a panic towards the end of the first week in July that year.

'Mr Rhea' – he sounded breathless on the phone – 'I've had rustlers, they've pinched all my Redpolls, the lot! Last night...'

'All of them?' I couldn't believe this. They must have had a fleet of cattle trucks to take them away, even if they had driven them on foot from the field.

'Aye, every one. All fifty-five.'

'I'll be there in ten minutes.'

When I arrived in Crampton I saw Sam pacing up and down the road outside his farm gate and went to join him. Mary, his daughter, was at his side and I could see the old fellow was very distressed. Mary was there to comfort him.

'So what's happened, Sam?' I asked.

'They were in yon field near t'river,' he said. 'Like they always are. Somebody's smashed t'gate down and taken all my cows. Every one of them's gone, vanished into thin air. A lifetime's work...'

'Show me,' I asked him.

We walked to the field in silence, with Mary coming along too, and soon I saw the field gate lying on the verge, smashed from its hinges. There were signs of hoofs all over the gateway, in the field, too, near the gate and between the woodwork of the gate, and then across the verge into the road beyond. And all along the road were dozens of fresh cowclaps with more hoofprints along the grass verges.

'Sam, I don't think they've been rustled,' I said. 'I think they've escaped. Look at that gate, it's lying outwards, smashed off its hinges, and the sneck has been knocked out. If a lorry or tractor had smashed into it, it would be lying inside the field, broken into bits, not lying outside in one piece on the verge. Something's pushed it from inside the field, Sam. And look at those cowclaps, there's a long trail of them... I think we should follow to see where they go.'

'Well, I'll be damned!' he muttered. 'You're right, Mr Rhea. I never noticed that. I should have, but I just thought we'd had thieves in the night but, aye, they've broken out! They'd only do that if they were scared, Mr Rhea, very scared of summat. So where in hangment can they be?'

'That's our next question. Have they done this before?'

'Nay, lad, never. Why would they want to break out of a lush grazing field like this?'

'They have broken out before, Dad,' Mary quietly corrected him. 'Not these same cows, but Grandad's herd did. In 1905. He told me about it years ago; it was long before I was born.'

'Aye, the lass is right, Mr Rhea, I'd forgotten about that. In my dad's day, it was, his herd smashed their way out of this same field, but this lot have never done so.'

'Grandad said it was just before the river flooded, Dad. He said the cows knew it was going to flood into their field, so they got out. And it did, so Grandad said; there was some kind of flash flood high on the moors and our river couldn't take it all. This field was awash in minutes, two or three feet deep.'

'She's right, Mr Rhea, my old dad often told us about that. Do you reckon the river's going to flood again, after all this time? I mean, cows wouldn't know that, would they?'

'That's something I can't answer, Sam,

although July can often produce flash floods and severe thunderstorms. But come along, we've a herd of cows to track down!'

We found them huddled together in woodland at the top of Crampton Bank, their route easy to follow due to the cow-claps on the road and their hoof marks in the verges and with Mary's help it was an easy task to drive them back into the village, a distance of about three-quarters of a mile. When they arrived at their former field, however, they refused to go in. Whatever had panicked them into a stampede through the gate was now compelling them not to return. Fortunately Sam was able to accommodate them in another of his fields on higher ground. They entered the new pasture quite happily and were soon calmly munching at the fresh new grass.

'I've never known this sort of thing happen to me, Mr Rhea,' said Sam later, over a cup of tea in his kitchen. 'Does it mean we're going to be flooded? I mean, there's no warning of heavy rain, is there?'

'The swallows have been flying low lately,' I said. 'And July can be stormy as you know, but this water comes down from the moors. It can be a different world up there, sending flood water down to us in no time. And you've got some scouts coming from Leeds, haven't you? Into this field?'

'In two or three days' time. I'd best warn them, eh? I've another field well away from the river they can use.'

And so the cows settled into their temporary new home. Sam rang the scout master from Leeds to say there had been a slight change of plan, and then he set about repairing the broken hinges and sneck of the demolished gate.

Four days later, that field was under two feet of very dirty river water due to unexpectedly severe flash floods which followed abnormally heavy rain.

The scouts would have had a very damp introduction to life in the countryside.

So, were the cows mysteriously aware of that impending flood, or was it nothing more than a coincidence and something else frightening the entire herd into a stampede?

In a similar vein, there are many stories of dogs being afraid of venturing into certain places, often those associated with ghosts or a past tragedy of some kind. It seems as if the animals are aware of something inexplicable lurking there. I've been told of dogs actually snarling at something beyond human comprehension. It makes one wonder if they can see or sense a presence which cannot be seen or felt by human beings. Similar tales are told about horses. In one village on my patch, there was a horse which utterly refused to cross a certain bridge and no one could understand why. Research into the history of the location showed that a woman had drowned there many years earlier, and her ghost was reputed to haunt the bridge. Other horses and dogs would happily make the crossing, so did that horse, like some humans, actually see a ghost or feel some kind of eerie presence which was not recognized by others? We shall never know.

Perhaps the most curious tale about such inexplicable things came to my attention when a lady resident of Maddleskirk rang to report her suspicions that someone was stealing racehorses. It happened regularly on moonlit nights and yet she had never seen anything. Her only experience, safe in the security of her house, was the regular sound of horses on the move. She had heard the rattling of their harnesses, their occasional neighing or metallic shaking of their bits, and the distinctive sound of their hoofs on the surface of the track.

When she rang me, I could sense she was

sincere in her report and so I went along to talk to her. I wanted to find out what it was all about, as I'd not received any reports of livestock being stolen in the district, although there were several racing stables nearby. She had specifically mentioned racehorses. So, if the owners or trainers of those racehorses had not reported any thefts, what was going on? Was there some kind of skulduggery involving switched racehorses, or drugging them before races? For all the oddity of the report, it meant I must unearth the truth.

Mrs Adele Henderson lived in an isolated stone cottage between Maddleskirk and Aidensfield, albeit with a Maddleskirk address. In her late fifties, she was a shop manager who worked in Ashfordly and was a widow, her husband having been killed in the Second World War. She had never remarried and there were no children of the marriage. She still lived in the house they'd bought as newly weds in the 1930s, a few years before the war. Her husband had been a chauffeur for a wealthy family in Maddleskirk and the cottage had once been owned by his employer. Henry Henderson had taken the opportunity to buy when they'd decided to sell, thus giving him, and his eventual widow, valuable security. It was rather isolated among trees and gorse bushes, but she loved it, and the couple had bought it because it was in such a quiet situation with wildlife all around them. Both were amateur naturalists and Mr Henderson had been a keen photographer of birds and animals; a lot of his work hung on her cottage walls.

The narrow lane between Maddleskirk and Aidensfield ran past the house, but the cosy building was set back off the highway to nestle in the hillside with wonderful views down the dale. As Mrs Henderson worked during the week, I arranged to see her on the Saturday evening after her phone call and she invited me in for a cup of tea and a scone.

'So, tell me about these stolen racehorses,' I said, after the inevitable incidental chat before we got down to the serious business.

'Well, I'm not really sure they are race-horses, Mr Rhea, because of the noise they make, the harness and bits rattling. Race-horses tend to be more quiet, don't they?'

'I suppose they do.' I was not really sure to be honest! 'But the noises you've heard? It was definitely horses?'

'Oh yes, there's no doubt about it, it's the noise of lots of horses on the move; my cat hears them too, she always lays her ears back and spits when we hear them. She hears them before I do and spits, then I know they're coming and can listen out for them.'

'But you've never seen them?'

'No. When I know that Susie has heard them, I go out to have a look but have never seen anything. It's very odd, Mr Rhea, and outside, of course, the noise is so much louder.'

'It's very puzzling, but I have to tell you I've not had any reports of horses being stolen, Mrs Henderson, not racehorses or horses of any other kind. So what makes you think they are being stolen?'

'It's always at midnight when there's a full moon, Mr Rhea. And there's always a lot of them on the move. The noise lasts for several minutes as they come past. It's always out of my sight which is why at first I thought somebody was stealing them. 'The noise is always so loud I can't ignore it, but I've never seen them. That's what makes me suspicious; they're obviously not using the road, they're being taken across country, in the shelter of the trees, bushes and hedges, well out of sight.'

'Not on the road which runs past your house?'

'No, I can see that road and they've never used it. Besides there'd be horse droppings on the road next morning, and there never is. I've been out to look.'

'If you've never seen anything, why do you think it's racehorses?'

'Only because there's a racing stable at the top of the hill behind my house, Mr Rhea, that's the only place nearby where there are lots of horses.'

'But there is no road, not even a bridle-path from the stables down here.'

'Exactly, Mr Rhea, which is why I thought they were being stolen and taken across country, down the hillside and past my house, then away down the dale.'

'As you know, Mrs Henderson, lots of people around here keep a horse and some have several, but there are no stables full of them, except the racing stables. It's very odd. I wonder if it's someone exercising horses by moonlight?'

'They'd use the road, Mr Rhea, but those horses don't.'

'A good point. Look, I'll make enquiries in the area to see if there's any explanation for a string of horses being moved at night. I'll let you know what I learn.'

In the days which followed, I visited every

horse owner in the locality, including the racing stables on the hilltop behind Mrs Henderson's cottage. It was situated more than a mile from her house with nothing between them but a stretch of moorland which dipped into the dale to become scrubland with trees and gorse bushes. The owner of the racing stables, Charles Whittam, assured me he'd not had any of his animals stolen and that he never exercised his horses late at night, certainly never by the light of the moon. He also stated he would not take expensive horses across the rough scrubland between his stables and Mrs Henderson's cottage in the dale below. There were too many risks of breaking delicate legs, or suffering other injuries on the rough terrain. Mr Whittam also explained that the security arrangements for his stables at night were extremely thorough; no one could illicitly remove a racehorse and certainly not a string of them, nor could they gain access for doping or other clandestine activities. He also assured me that when racehorses were being exercised, they did not produce the same sounds as, say, a team of heavy horses which, according to my version of her experience, corresponded with the noise heard by Mrs Henderson. Mr Whittam felt that her account sounded more like an army on the move, not a string of racehorses in training.

Mrs Henderson's odd experience remained a mystery and I began to wonder if she was imagining the entire episode; her only witness was her cat and I could not question an animal as a witness! In spite of my reservations, I felt her account had a strong ring of truth about it, otherwise she would not have contacted me.

The curious matter might have remained unresolved had Miss Leonora Holden not lost her camera. Leonora, a lady in her mid-sixties, lived in Aidensfield and was a professional author, specializing in historical works, both fact and fiction. She was an authority on the history of the district and used her camera to back up her researches. On this occasion, she had been examining some medieval ruins on the moors near Eltering and when she returned home, realized she must have left her camera behind. She had hurried back to the site to make a search but there was no sign of it, so she had reported her loss to the police in the hope someone had found it and handed it in. And so they had. An honest visitor had found it in the ruins and handed it to Eltering Police; it had been sent along to me so that I could return it to Leonora against her signature.

She insisted I join her for a cup of coffee and some biscuits because she loved to question me about my work, and enjoyed some of the stories I could tell. I am sure she used some in her novels. As we chatted, she asked if I'd had any interesting experiences in recent months and I decided to mention the mysterious horses which moved by moonlight. I provided an account without mentioning Mrs Henderson by name and Leonora smiled and nodded as I related the tale.

'It's the Roman army on the move,' she told me. 'There used to be a Roman road which ran past the site of those racing stables and into the dale. It started up in North-umberland and came this way, using high ground wherever possible, then descended into the dale near that cottage where Adele Henderson lives. Then it crossed the dale and continued south. They've been heard before, you know, many times but always in moonlight. Some Romans moved at night, you see, by the light of the moon but your witness – Mrs Henderson at a guess – will never see them, She'll hear them, just as her cat does, but don't ask me whether it's ghosts or if there is any other explanation. I don't know. All I know is that down the years people have heard an army of horses moving in that part of the dale, always at full moon. There's absolutely nothing left of that old road, not even a bridleway or footpath but the route used to be shown on some very old maps. All I can say is that some things happen which may never be explained.'

When I told Adele Henderson she was very pleased if a trifle nervous at the notion that an army of ghostly horses might be passing her house on moonlit occasions but she never mentioned them again. And neither did her cat.

Chapter 6

As I patrolled my patch during the summer when our beautiful part of England was alive with day-trippers and tourists, there was one double-barrelled question which was repeatedly asked by visitors. It was this, even if it was phrased in different ways: what do all these country people do for a living and how do they occupy themselves when they're not working? Variations might be:

How do they manage to earn enough to survive, living out here on the moors? Why are there so many smart cars in these country villages when there aren't any offices or factories to work in? Do they drive into town to work, because there aren't any factories, offices or shops out here, and where is the nearest cinema or theatre? What on earth do they do for entertainment after work, especially in winter? Where do they do their shopping? How do they manage without buses or street lights?

The way of life of ordinary country people puzzled our friends from the cities and towns, and I must admit the same questions sometimes occurred to me. Several of the people on my beat appeared to live very well indeed without any visible means of support. I reasoned that quite a lot lived in houses which had belonged to their parents or grandparents, being passed down the generations over the years. That meant there would be no rent or mortgage, a wonderful bonus for someone with children and, of course, the furniture and fittings were also handed down. If such family-owned houses required any repairs or maintenance, then it would be done by the man of the house.

Another factor, particularly among the

menfolk, was that they rarely, if ever, bought new clothes. Even for important events like weddings and funerals, they would wear a suit, shirt, shoes and hat handed down by their father and grandfather which might explain why so many family photographs always looked rather dated. Such outfits were always 'kept for best' which meant they were only worn on Sundays (and then not every Sunday) and on other occasions during a person's lifetime such as weddings or funerals. Some suits, which inevitably smelt of mothballs, could be more than fifty years old, often with no signs of wear and tear, and good for many more years to come. Certainly, they would be made of the best materials, one rural logic being that it is cheaper in the long term to buy good quality goods even if they seem to be very expensive at the outset. Women might also wear dresses handed down through the generations although many were capable needlewomen who could mend or make their own, or even create a smart new outfit from their mother's old clothes. Countrywomen were rather more fashion conscious than their menfolk.

Also most of the houses in a village, especially the older ones, had considerable areas of land attached to them which was never allowed to be wasted; it had to be productive and was seldom, if ever, used for recreation. Leisure activities like sunbathing, or playing games in the garden were rarely indulged in because the garden's purpose was to produce fruit and vegetables in sufficient quantities to cope with the family's need throughout the coming year. Tending the garden was a skilled task, being both important and time consuming. Invariably, one part of a rural garden was set aside for livestock because most families kept hens, ducks or geese. There might be rabbits, too, and at least one pig, all sources of food. When the pig was killed and cured, it would keep the family in ham and bacon for almost the entire year. Bigger families kept more livestock and probably more pigs, while some even ran to a cow in milk or perhaps a goat. Food and income were generated by such livestock.

In short, it was this kind of necessary self-sufficiency, accompanied by the inevitable hard work, which enabled people to live in villages on very small incomes – they did not need money for expensive outside entertainment, for travelling to work, for new clothes, or indeed for the upkeep or purchase of their houses. And, of course, they could earn a few extra shillings by selling eggs, fruit or vegetables, or doing odd jobs for others, even to the extent of taking in washing or doing the ironing for ageing villagers.

Few rural people held bank accounts, except perhaps a savings account in the village post office. Almost all their business and personal dealings were in cash; few borrowed money because getting into debt was considered unworthy and dangerous. Their money was kept in the house, usually hidden, and from a police perspective this was unwise due to the risk of theft. Happily, there were few thieves about at that time, perhaps because the crime of burglary carried a maximum sentence of life imprisonment. A person's home was indeed his or her castle and burglary was very rare. If money was stolen from private houses, it was usually in small amounts taken by sneak thieves from purses left visible and accessible on kitchen tables and window ledges.

Even if many villagers lived this kind of life, some had reasonable incomes because they were shopkeepers such as butchers or grocers, others were dressmakers or tailors, hairdressers or barbers, plumbers or electricians, carpenters, wheelwrights, undertakers, farriers and blacksmiths, none of which might be a full-time occupation. I knew a porter at a railway station who also ran a smallholding, and my own grandfather was an innkeeper, farmer and water bailiff. Quite often a man needed more than one source of income, particularly if he had a young family. There were motor mechanics, painters and decorators, builders, cobblers, innkeepers, insurance men, clergymen, doctors and, of course, policemen, all serving one small community and often running smallholdings or small businesses as sidelines. In most cases, therefore, the villagers did not need to go into town to do their shopping or seek the help of the service industries – they had everything literally on the doorstep.

Even in the 1960s, there were old people who had never been away from their home village, not even for a day. There is a lovely 1960s story of an elderly widow being taken for her first ride in a car. She lived in Wensleydale, one of the most beautiful of the Yorkshire Dales, and her grandson took her up the Buttertubs pass, parking on the hilltop which separates Wensleydale from glorious Swaledale. Looking down into the expanse of Swaledale, the old lady said, 'I never knew the world was such a big place.'

Similarly, I once stopped to chat with an elderly character sitting on a bench outside a moorland inn. He lost no time telling me he was ninety-two years old, and when I asked if he had lived in the village all his life, he said, 'Aye, I have, but I once went away.'

'Where did you go?' I asked.

'Northallerton,' he said. 'It was market-day.'

Northallerton is about five miles from where he had lived all his life.

On another occasion, a young village lad decided he wanted to get away from his home village and seek work elsewhere. After a lot of consideration, he opted for Canada and after he'd gone, two old men were discussing him when one asked, 'How did young Matthew get to Canada?' The other replied, 'He went over that hill,' pointing up to the moor. And I love the story of a tourist in the moors who said to a local, 'What a lovely sunset!' 'Aye, said the local, 'it's not bad for a small village like this.'

But things were destined to change. Those of us who can remember the Second World War will recall the swift-moving changes which followed the victory celebrations, for it was then that village life began to alter with increasing speed. With the disappearance of wartime austerity, townspeople decided it would be nice to live in a village and travel to work, and so new houses were built with smaller gardens, council estates appeared in some villages, the inns became busier, some being altered to fit the image of the incomers, and that host of long-time self-employed people began to find fresh riches among waves of new residents even if some professions were on the decline. If farriers found their work dwindling, then garages were taking their place; if washerwomen were no longer required, washing-machine servicemen were needed instead. If the village tailor was redundant, shops now sold ready-to-wear clothes. The post-war changes to rural England were massive, even if they were not recognized as such at the time.

I arrived in Aidensfield some twenty years after the end of the Second World War, at a time when changes to the rural way of life were very evident. I just missed the era when village constables rode around on pedal cycles for I was allocated an official motor cycle which was soon replaced by a Mini-van complete with official police radio. Those sort of changes affected my own little world, but in the villages on my patch, the changes were more drastic. Several shops had disappeared, the railways had closed and yet commuters were living in Aidensfield and travelling long distances to work by car. Village handymen found themselves out of work because things didn't need to be repaired or 'fettled' – instead, new parts were fitted to household equipment by firms which offered guarantees. The old way of village life was being eradicated; the days of cheap and contented living were quickly disappearing.

In spite of the changes, however, true village people continued to be just as entrepreneurial as they had always been, finding work where none existed and earning themselves extra cash, often without leaving the area.

One such man was Malcolm Rudge known to everyone as Mudge. He was a bachelor in his late fifties and all the time I had known him, he'd never had a proper job. I often wondered how he earned his daily bread although he lived in a cottage handed down by his parents and had a large garden in which he grew very good vegetables and soft fruit which he sold at his gate. He was also capable of turning his hand to most tasks needed by the new breed of householder, like cleaning drains and gutters, trimming hedges, cutting lawns and even doing a spot of painting and decorating. He worked for cash which meant the tax man did not interfere with his money-making schemes. In spite of his modest existence, Mudge ran a fine new car, a green Morris Traveller which cost something around £500 at that time. Clearly, he was doing very well without a regular job. Naturally, as a policeman, I wondered how he could afford a new vehicle. Many a thief or confidence trickster has been unmasked thanks to policemen being suspicious about their earning capacity and their openly enjoyed unusually expensive tastes.

Even if Mudge was not declaring his earnings to the Inland Revenue, I thought the income he scratched from his various but irregular enterprises was not sufficient to buy and run such a nice vehicle and yet I knew he was not a criminal. He was not a thief, neither was he a confidence trickster and I was fairly certain he was not a blackmailer or bank robber, and to my knowledge, he'd not come into money from a deceased relative, or by winning the football pools. Mudge was quite careful with his money and I guessed he might have substantial savings tucked away but men like that, with savings hidden in the house, did not splash out on brand new cars.

They hated spending money and kept their growing pile of cash for the proverbial rainy day, or to help in their old age.

Nonetheless, I decided that a discreet observation would be a good idea because I did not want to suggest to him openly, or to anyone else, that because I thought his lifestyle appeared to exceed his income, he was conducting his life beyond the border-lines of legality. Avoiding the payment of income tax was not considered illegal – indeed, some said it was the national sport. On the other hand, *evading* income tax would be seen in a different light!

During my highly discreet observation, I discovered that Mudge left the village each morning just after seven in his car. He drove out towards Ashfordly and I wondered if he actually had an early-morning job of some kind because he always returned before ten o'clock usually to resume work on his small-holding. If he did not return to his smallhold-ing, he would take care of one or other of his multifarious tasks, invariably fairly close to Aidensfield. Wondering what he could be doing in Ashfordly at that time of day, I made a point of remembering to see if I could spot him next time I paid an early visit to the town. His car would be easy to find, therefore its location might provide a clue.

The outcome of that little exercise showed that he did not stop in Ashfordly on every occasion; sometimes he continued down the dale to either Brantsford or even further on to Eltering. Both were busy market towns, Brantsford being about the size of Ashfordly and Eltering being marginally larger and busier. Each time, however, it was an early outing which allowed him to return home by mid-morning and it didn't take me long to discover that his trips coincided with the market-days in those towns. Eltering's market was on a Monday, Brantsford's on a Wednesday and Ashfordly's on a Friday. So was he doing nothing more sinister than taking produce into town for sale to stall-holders at the markets? That was exactly the kind of thing I would expect him to do because fresh fruit, vegetables and eggs were always in demand. But that didn't explain his other outings to those towns which were on Tuesdays, Thursdays and Saturdays, non-market-days and apparently done randomly, although I discovered he did not undertake such trips on Sundays. I began to think it was silly to suspect him of some kind of skulduggery because I realized he was doing exactly what a countryman would do – selling the result of his labours to those who wanted to buy it. That was how these country folk lived without having proper jobs. With that realization, I began to lose interest in the puzzle I had created for myself – I concluded Mudge was nothing but a hardworking and very successful self-employed countryman.

And then one Monday morning while I was undertaking an early patrol of the entire sub-division in Ashfordly section's Ford Anglia, I spotted Mudge's familiar car parked near a bus stop. It was on the outskirts of Eltering on one of the main roads into town and the time was 8.15. There were no passengers at the bus stop, but Mudge was wandering around it, peering at the ground as if looking for something. He did not notice me and because I had an appointment to keep, I did not stop for a chat.

In isolation, that little incident meant nothing but later that morning, a few minutes after nine o'clock when I was on foot patrol in Eltering and in deep discussion with the inspector about a forthcoming court case in which I was a witness, I saw Mudge again. On this occasion he was also pottering inside a bus shelter and peering at the ground. As before, I thought he must have lost something, but in a bus shelter? He was travelling by car! This bus shelter was in the town centre, not far from the market-place and nowhere near the car-park. Because I was with Inspector Breckon I didn't approach Mudge. It was market-day and the town was busy. The market-place in particular was crowded with early morning shoppers and stallholders, the daily rush of workers having now disappeared into their offices, shops and factories.

Very spasmodically over the next few weeks, I spotted Mudge in more bus shelters, always fairly early in the morning on market-days in Eltering, Brantsford or Ashfordly but I also came across him on other days in those towns, always walking around in circles near bus stops or in bus shelters. By this stage, of course, that is where I looked for him – I now knew that if I wanted to see Mudge at work, I had to be in the vicinity of a bus shelter or bus stop. Some were in the town centres, others on the outskirts and some in the suburbs, but the prime time for Mudge spotting was usually between 8.15 and 9.15.

It follows that my curiosity about his odd

activities began to increase and I am sure he never noticed me in the assorted police vehicles I used because he was too intent on the task in hand. I did not like to appear nosy by asking him outright: I had to contain my interest in his morning activity which, to my knowledge, was no kind of law-breaking.

However, one of my duties, on very infrequent occasions, was to undertake office duty at Eltering when there was a shortage of manpower. This happened when the town's regular constables were taken from their duties for other work, such as court appearances, race meetings, courses of various kinds, first-aid training and so forth. On those occasions, it was sometimes necessary to draft in officers from elsewhere within the sub-division, if only for a spell of, say, a couple of hours in the office to cope with telephone calls and visitors. By chance, I was doing one of those sessions in Eltering Police Station one Monday morning between 9 a.m. and 11 a.m.

Just after 9.15, Mudge walked in, his face registering surprise when he saw me.

'Oh, hello, Mr Rhea, I didn't know you got this far from home on a morning!'

I explained how Ashfordly and Aidensfield were part of Eltering Sub-Division, and that with our increased mobility we were occasionally expected to patrol the whole area, not just those parts near our base.

'So what can I do for you, Mudge?' Everyone called him Mudge and so I was not being rude!

'I've come to report finding this.' He plonked a £1 note on the counter.

'Fair enough.' I lifted the Found Property Register from its place under the counter and opened it to enter details. Before doing so, I checked the Lost Property Register, but no one had reported losing the pound note.

I then recorded his name and address, the date and place of finding which he said was the market-place in Eltering, and told him that he should retain the money. If it was not claimed within three months, it would become his property. Should the loser report the loss, however, Mudge would have to repay it.

'Aye, I know the routine, Mr Rhea,' he smiled. 'The lads in here have explained it all, that's why I report all finds over ten bob.'

'Why ten shillings?' I frowned.

'Well, folks who lose the small stuff, like pennies, three-penny bits and sixpences, even shillings and half crowns, aren't likely to report it. If they lose small coins, they'll say goodbye to them, especially if they're rushing on to a bus to get to work, so I was told those little coins can be considered abandoned. And you can't be nicked for stealing stuff that's been abandoned by its owner, so I was told. But folks might just report losing summat like a ten-bob note, or a pound, certainly a fiver – not that many folks lose fivers. That's why I'm reporting this one, just to keep myself on the right side of the law.'

As he was speaking, I recalled seeing him apparently looking for things at bus stops and in bus shelters. Was he deliberately looking for lost money?

'Mudge,' I said, 'are you telling me you go around deliberately looking for money in bus shelters and at bus stops?'

'Been doing it for years, Mr Rhea, ever since I was a schoolboy. I realized that when folks are waiting for buses they ferret around for the right money in small change, and often lose some of it just as the bus is coming in. They never bother to pick it up because they're too keen to get on board, so I go around and collect it. There's good money in bus shelters, Mr Rhea, just waiting to be picked up. I do it on a morning, that's when folks are queuing to get to work or wanting to get to market while they're loaded down with baskets and bags. They can't be bothered with looking for their lost coins if they're only pennies and tanners.'

'So how much do you find each week?'

'It varies, Mr Rhea. One very good week I found thirty quid in all, most of it in shillings and two-bob bits, but generally it's more like five quid. Not bad for a couple of hours' work. It's brought me in two or three hundred quid a year. You've got to get to the bus stop just after the queue's got on board and before the next queue starts to form, otherwise they'll find the cash ... it's quite an art, Mr Rhea. I've got to know the local timetables by heart, but ever since I was a lad, I've put that money aside. My dad told me to do that, he said it was manna from heaven, and it would keep me when I get old ... but recently I worked out I had enough to get myself a nice car, so I can visit more bus stops now ... it's just a hobby, you understand. I'll soon earn enough to replace that car money and put a bit aside for my old age. But I do like to keep it all above the law. Mind you, with more folks buying cars, there's less money being lost at bus stops, but on the other hand, folks are losing bigger amounts. Where you might have got somebody losing a threepenny bit a few years back, nowadays they might drop a shilling. As a matter of interest, telephone kiosks are another good place for finding dropped money...'

He seemed quite prepared to tell me all about his rather odd money-making scheme and I found nothing illegal about it. If anyone went to Mudge to say they'd lost some money at one of his regular visiting places, he would cheerfully refund it, but people didn't behave like that. If they lost a small amount of cash, like a penny, three-penny bit or even a shilling while hurrying to board a bus, they would almost certainly consider it lost for ever.

'I'll tell you summat, though, Mr Rhea,' he said, as he turned to leave. 'The folks of Ash-fordly aren't ones for dropping much. The only stuff I find at their stops or in their shelters is small coppers, pennies more often than not. I don't do very well in Ashfordly, but Brantsford isn't too bad. I once found a pound note there; it was never claimed.'

'That explains why you've not been into Ashfordly Police Station to report your finds!'

'Aye, you're right. I can't remember the last time I was in there, probably soon after Blaketon arrived, I reckon. It was years ago but I found a pound note in that bus shelter near Ryegate. It wasn't claimed either. But as for here in Eltering, well, it seems these folks have money to chuck away!'

As he left the police station to continue his work, I wondered how many more Mudges there were in the country. And I wondered how much cash is abandoned in Britain's streets every day. Enough to buy a few new cars, I should think.

Undoubtedly, Mudge had found a neat way of earning a few extra pounds just as many country people found ways of adding to their income by scouring the landscape for free fruit and vegetables. For example, people picked and sold fresh mushrooms, crab apples, sloes, hazel nuts, brambles, sweet chestnuts and herbs of various kinds, all collected at no charge and sold for a few shillings. I knew a man who collected hazel rods and fashioned walking sticks or shepherds' crooks from them; a woman went around picking up particularly nicely shaped stones, then painting them in the form of animals, and selling them as door stops.

Another collected wild flowers which she dried and made into pictures rather like paintings.

There were dozens of ways of earning extra cash from what was available in the countryside, and the principle was similar to that practised by Mudge in that many things were available free of charge if only one was prepared to make an effort to find them, and then develop some means of capitalizing upon that discovery.

A few months after talking to Mudge, I came across a man who had developed that kind of hunting skill into a highly professional operation. I hadn't encountered him earlier because he did not live in my beat although he lived within the boundaries of Eltering Sub-Division. It was during another of my spells of duty patrolling the area around Eltering that I first met him. It was Inspector Breckon who asked me to carry out a small duty.

'Ah, PC Rhea, just the fellow.' The inspector was an affable character who was popular with his subordinates. 'I've a nice little job for you.'

He explained that he had received a telephone call from a gentleman called Ralph Lofthouse who lived at Dale House, Pattington which was not far from Eltering. It seemed that Mr Lofthouse was thinking of selling cider from his premises and had contacted the police to determine the correct procedure, such as getting the necessary excise licence and coping with licensing hours. Because, on the face of things, it seemed a rather odd request, the inspector felt I should drive out to interview Mr Lofthouse, which would also allow me to assess the premises. Inspector Breckon said he did not think Lofthouse was considering a restaurant or public house at his premises, and wondered why he would suddenly decide he wanted to sell cider. Inspector Breckon told me I was expected that morning by Mr Lofthouse, and I said I would drive out straight away to discover what I could.

After a twenty-minute drive, I found myself motoring along a very narrow, unsurfaced lane with several passing places along the half-mile route, and then arrived at a neat stone-built house set in its own grounds. My first impression was that the grounds were full of symmetrical rows of small trees and it didn't look anything like a garden. Its appearance was rather more like parkland. I halted outside a gate which bore the name of the place and went in. As I approached the house, I saw a handwritten sign saying, 'We're in the shed, turn left and follow the footpath.'

I obeyed and soon found myself approaching a stone-built outhouse the rear of which backed on to a high wall of the kind which enclosed the walled gardens of Victorian times. The door was standing open and, as I approached, a young woman emerged and welcomed me.

'Hello, I'm Rebecca, Ralph's wife. He's in there – just go in. Can I get you a cup of coffee and a chocolate biscuit?'

'Lovely,' I enthused, and walked into the building which reminded me of a cross between a potting shed and an office. A tall, slender man was doing something to plants on what looked like a large metal-topped table.

'Hello,' I called. 'I'm PC Rhea from Aidensfield. Inspector Breckon from Eltering asked me to call.'

'That didn't take long!' The man halted his activities and came towards me, hand outstretched. I shook it. Immediately, I decided he was a likeable and trustworthy fellow; in his early forties, I estimated, slender and lithe, with a good head of dark hair and smiling eyes. 'I just rang a few minutes ago!'

'I happened to be in the area,' I said. 'So what can I do for you?'

'Come through to the office end,' he invited, and I followed him through a door at the end of the shed, and into another area containing a low table and three old chairs. There were flowers in the window ledge and pictures hanging from the walls, definitely a feminine touch, I thought. 'This is my entertaining suite,' he grinned, inviting me to sit down. 'Rebecca will bring the coffee in here.'

As I settled down, we chatted about the weather and incidental things such as the wonderful situation this house occupied.

The coffee arrived but Rebecca did not remain and, as we enjoyed it, I asked, 'Well, Mr Lofthouse, what's this about wanting to sell cider? It doesn't look as if you've got potential public-house premises here!'

'Oh, no, I don't want to run a pub or an off-licence, not even a restaurant; well, not at this stage. No, Mr Rhea, this is an orchard.'

'Ah!' I said. 'That explains those rows of trees I spotted when I arrived.'

'Right, they're apple trees. I have sixty-three acres here, Mr Rhea, all in a very sheltered location well off the moors and away from the most severe weather. We've almost got our own micro-climate which is why it's such a good place to grow apples. I have more than seven hundred trees and dozens of varieties. It's my full-time occupation and I believe this is the most northerly commercial orchard in England.'

'I wouldn't have thought apples would be commercially successful this far north,' I said. 'I've always associated apples with Kent and Herefordshire, or France, not the northerly part of Yorkshire.'

'We grow specialist varieties on dwarf trees, including some rare ones,' he said. 'We're not seeking to look pretty with handsome trees full of blossom for people to admire, but simply to grow good tasty English apples. I hope to increase our number of rare varieties, and already we've quite a collection. I know some orchards with up to two hundred varieties, but we'll be content with something less than that. We shall soon be opening to the public, selling apples at the gate and inviting customers to tour the premises, and of course, continuing to take bulk orders from shops.'

'And so your own brand of cider is a logical extension of your enterprise?'

'Right; along with other apple-associated products like books of recipes, picture postcards and even apple peelers, core removers, seedlings and home storage units! I'm not open to the public just yet which is why there aren't any signs outside the premises, but we hope to start this coming autumn, when the apples are ripe. Our first planted trees are mature now and producing good crops which we already sell to shops, others will follow next year, until the whole orchard is productive. But this year will be the first time we've invited the public into our orchard. Along with the other merchandise I've mentioned, I thought our own cider would be a useful addition to our sales.'

'I agree, but you might need planning permission if the public is going to come down that lane,' I warned him. 'And warning signs to tell people they're emerging on to a busy road when they leave.'

'That's all in hand, we're going to widen the lane. Our solicitor is looking into all that, but he said I should first contact the police about the liquor licence.'

I asked whether he intended selling his cider for consumption on his orchard premises and he said, 'No, we might think of a small café or tea rooms later, in which case we might want customers to enjoy a glass, but not at this stage. All we want now is for customers to buy our bottles of cider and take them home or give them away as presents.'

I explained he would have to visit the Magistrates' Clerk in Eltering to apply for an excise licence which would permit him to manufacture the cider for commercial sales, and then he would need a justices' off-licence which would allow him to sell it for consumption, but only off the premises. Once the application was made, the police would make a formal inspection of the premises and check the character of the applicant and, all being well, the licences would be approved quickly. So far as I knew, I said, the hours during which he could sell his cider would be the same as off-licences in town, i.e. throughout the day from 8.30 a.m. until 10.30 p.m. except on Sundays when the hours would be same as for inns and other on-licensed premises in the locality. In case he wanted to check things for himself, I told him the relevant legislation was the Licensing Act of 1964 which had recently relaxed some of the rules relating to intoxicants.

After one or two questions, he asked if I would like to see his orchard and with Rebecca alongside, I was treated to a guided tour. It was neatly laid out on mown grass with hundreds of trees being supported by stakes. None of the trees was more than ten feet high and some were much smaller, still in their comparative youth. He explained how his father had started the orchard in the firm belief it could become commercially viable if he concentrated on rare and specialist species; in the coming months, the first of the trees would produce the first crop for his new customers.

As we strolled around, he mentioned the names of some apples, which I must admit meant nothing to me – names like Jupiter, Ribston Pippin, Peasgood's Nonsuch, Bloody Butcher, Sheep's Nose, Catshead, Jonathan, Norfolk Beefing and Minnesota Russet all dripped from his tongue – although I did recognize some, such as Beauty of Bath, Granny Smith and Golden Delicious.

'So if these are rare or specialist apples, where did you find the trees?' I asked.

'Dad found a lot along the side of railway lines,' he said in all seriousness. 'And I continued to find them there, but with Dr Beeching's efforts to close rural lines, that source has dried up to a large extent. We were established just before it happened, fortunately. Mind you, some railway lines are still open so we'll probably find more if we look, and the verges of our roads and lanes are a good source except where the grass is cut regularly. Council grasscutters chop down a lot of seedlings. Picnic areas in the National Park are a good source too. Sometimes we find only a core with pips in, but sometimes we do find young trees growing...'

'You mean you just go out and find rare specimens?'

'It's the best way, Mr Rhea. And the cheapest! People throw apple cores out of trains and cars, or toss them away when they're having a picnic, and so we collect them. We know where to look. Most of them have the pips still inside and when they've got bits of skin still on them it helps to identify them.'

'Good grief! I suppose tons must be thrown away every day!' I exclaimed.

'Right, hundreds of tons more like! We can't collect them all but you'd be amazed at how many rare apples find themselves reduced to cores and then tossed away beside rail tracks or roads. People have no idea what they're eating. Sometimes we find a little tree, only a few inches tall, so we'll rescue it for our orchard.'

'And so you bring the cores or trees here and nurture them?'

'Absolutely right, although we are quite selective. It takes a long time to identify a species from a tiny plant and so we have a corner, that one just over to your right, our nursery, where they grow until they can be recognized. It's much easier to look at the skin left on a fresh core, then we can name almost every core we find! We'll sell any seedlings we don't want because I think there is a market for unusual species of apple trees, although obviously a lot are very common. By and large, if we want to expand with more varieties, we'll continue to rely heavily on our pickings from railway and road verges and, of course, we'll continue to expand using our own seeds. But there are apples galore out there, just waiting to be collected! I might add it's done with per-mission of the railway authorities although we don't need the same authority to collect from the roadside or picnic sites.'

'A variety of the famous hedgerow har-vest?' was all I could think of saying. 'Thanks for the tour. I'll tell my inspector that yours is a well-thought-out commercial venture and I'm sure he'll want to come out for a look.'

'He's more than welcome, and thanks for your advice.'

'Now I know what to do with my apple cores!' I said, as I turned to leave.

'Moon-washed apples of wonder,' he smiled. 'That's going to be our slogan.'

All I could think of saying in response was, 'Well, if my children ever want an apple for their teacher, I know where to come.'

'So long as they don't give her a Pomme d'Enfer,' he chuckled, as we said our fare-wells. 'That's known as the apple from Hell; you should see what it does to peoples' faces when they try to eat it. Better to give her a Kidd's Red Orange which is in fact an apple.'

As I drove away, I wondered how many other orchards were based on this kind of core cultivation and then, as I drove down the road back to Eltering, I wondered where else would anyone find so many discarded apple cores? In his way, I realized, he was helping to keep Britain tidy and it was a wonderful way of recycling someone else's cast-offs.

Chapter 7

Dogs of all shapes, colours, sizes and breeds are an integral part of country life, being used both as companions and workmates, in addition to those bred only for hunting and show purposes. It is not surprising there are many laws relating to them and, during my time at Aidensfield, doggy legislation covered everything from cruelty to boarding establishments. There were laws about collars, licences, the worrying of livestock, strays, rabies, dangerous dogs, accidents involving motor vehicles and even rewards for the recovery of stolen dogs. It was an offence, for example, to corruptly take any reward under pretence or upon account of aiding any person to recover any stolen dog. I have no idea why Parliament saw fit to make this a specific offence but it appeared in the Larceny Act of 1916, section 5(3), which was in force until 1968, covering the period I was at Aidensfield. I have to say I never dealt with such an offence.

I have recounted many tales of dogs in previous *Constable* books and there are probably hundreds more which could be told, but here is just another small selection. The first concerns a wandering dog which caused several traffic accidents. No one could catch it or identify its owner, and no one seemed to know where it had come from, or how long it had been roaming. There was a suggestion it was living wild, although we'd had no reports of raids on poultry, rabbits, butchers' shops or even domestic kitchens or dust-bins. If the number of traffic accidents along with their widely spread venues were any guide, it was clearly roaming across a huge tract of countryside in and around Ashfordly and Aidensfield. In spite of frequent sightings and accident reports, the only description we could muster was that it was 'a biggish black dog, about the size of a labrador.'

The first time I encountered anyone who had actually seen the mysterious animal was when I received a radio call one lunchtime to say a van had run off the road between Aidensfield and Elsinby. It had gone into a ditch, but the driver was not badly hurt, suffering only a few cuts and bruises. However, as he had demolished a few yards of railings and a reflecting post which was there to warn motorists of the impending corner, it was necessary to formally report the accident. The nearby farmer, owner of the railings in question, had rung me because he'd come across the hapless man in the ditch moments after it had happened, and so I drove to the scene in my official Mini-van.

When I arrived, I saw it was Alec Moore, a thirty-something self-employed gardener-cum-handyman who lived in Elsinby. He toured the district in his van which was always loaded with gardening tools, a wheel-barrow, lawnmower, hose pipe, apparently endless balls of string and rope, pruning shears and a host of other necessities. He never considered himself a real gardener because he knew nothing of the names or habits of flowers or vegetables, but he could keep a garden well tended and clean if he was told precisely what to do – and what not to do. He had been known to cut down valu-able decorative shrubs because he thought he was pruning them. He was fairly good at cutting lawns and hedges, and removing rubbish, especially that which he generated.

However, his van now had its front wheels in a ditch and its bonnet through a farmer's railings with Alec himself patiently awaiting my arrival. The farmer was there too, a man called Walter Baker from High Barns Farm at Elsinby. It was evident that Alec did not require medical attention, and so the accident was not serious.

'Now then, Mr Rhea.' Walter came to meet me as I parked nearby. 'He'll have to pay to get that fence fixed, you know, I don't want my cows straying through it.'

'No problem, Mr Baker,' said Alec. 'I'm comprehensively insured, they'll see to it.'

'Aye, but when? I need it done now.'

'The van's doing a good job of blocking the hole, the cows can't get out,' I said. 'So let's get the details from you both and then we can sort out the business of getting the fence fixed.'

The pair knew one another and I knew both quite well. One of the tasks of a village constable was to know the personalities living on one's patch and I was a regular visitor to Walter Baker's farm. I had to check his stock register at least once every three months and regarded him as a very decent and sensible man. I did not know Alec quite so well for I'd only a few professional dealings with him, but he was one of the regulars in the Hopbind Inn at Elsinby, being a member of the darts team. On this occasion, there was no suggestion Alec had been drinking and I could not smell alcohol on his breath, so I had no reason to suspect it contributing to this mishap.

With the two men in patient attendance, I recorded the necessary details, measured the road for the inevitable sketch I would have to produce, sought signs of skid marks, or some other reason for Alec's van to go into the ditch, and inspected the van for obvious defects such as a puncture. In such cases, there was always the possibility of prosecuting the driver for careless driving, or perhaps a more serious offence even though no other vehicle was involved, and so I had to compile my accident report with that in mind.

When eventually I submitted my report through the sergeant at Ashfordly, he would scrutinize it to see whether a prosecution was necessary. He would make his recommendations and forward the file to the inspector at Sub-Division who would do likewise before sending it to the superintendent at Divisional Headquarters for a final decision. Inevitably, the question would arise as to why the van had run off the road, particularly as no other vehicle was involved. A vehicle did not normally veer off the road unless there was a sound reason – a tyre suddenly bursting, icy conditions, swerving to avoid another vehicle or person, steering failure or even the driver falling asleep at the wheel. They were all typical reasons and perhaps excuses. And, of course, there was always the question of the driver being under the influence of either alcohol or drugs or falling ill. I had no reason to suspect Alec of any of those conditions, but was duty bound to establish what had happened.

'It was that black dog,' he said with all seriousness. 'It shot out of the hedge and ran right across the road just in front of me. I didn't stand a chance, Mr Rhea. I swerved and finished up in that ditch.'

'And the dog?' I asked. 'What happened to it?'

'Search me.' He shrugged his shoulders. 'I didn't hit it and never saw it again. Mind, it took me a few seconds to gather my wits before I got out of the van ... it had plenty of time to escape.'

'Any idea who it belongs to?'

'No idea, but it's probably that one that's been seen around the place recently. A few of my mates have had nasty scares with it suddenly dashing across the road.'

'Ah, *that* black dog!' I recalled the various accounts of the black labrador type of dog which was apparently living wild in the district. Now, it would appear, it had decided to operate on my beat! I hoped I could find it before it caused any more trouble.

'Well, I've never seen it,' said Farmer Baker. 'And I live right here. Where's it come from?'

'We don't know,' I told Walter. 'According to our reports, there's been one or two sightings in and around Ashfordly, usually by motorists. It's a black dog rather like a labrador, but no one's ever caught it or seen it with anyone. And we've no reports of a dog being lost. Now it seems it's come here.'

There was a school of thought which suggested a driver should not swerve to avoid an animal in the road, the logic being that it was dangerous to other road users, and that an animal's life was not so precious as that of a human being. In swerving to avoid an animal, a driver could be seriously injured or, of course, another driver might be harmed in some way. In the country, the carcasses of many wild creatures bear testimony to that belief – birds of every kind, especially pheasants, are frequent victims of traffic accidents, while hedgehogs, rabbits, moles, squirrels, frogs, toads, cats, foxes, deer and badgers are killed in massive quantities. It can be argued that such deaths are now a part of the natural cycle of life because those carcasses provide food for other creatures. Scavengers like crows, magpies and even foxes reap rich pickings from the victims of road traffic accidents.

There is no obligation to report such accidents to the police. Only if the following animals are injured or killed by a motor vehicle do the police have to be informed – dog, goat, cattle, horse, ass, mule, pig or sheep. There is no obligation to report a collision with an elephant, ape, giraffe, antelope, cat or a mouse – or any other creature apart from the eight which are listed.

'If that dog's running wild, it'll have to be stopped,' grunted Walter. 'If it comes near my sheep or hens, it can expect me to get my gun out!'

I felt this was not the time or place to remind Walter of the law relating to the shooting of dogs caught in the act of worrying livestock, but having obtained all the necessary information for my report, including a rough estimate of the value of the damaged fence and a note of the minor damage to the van, I said, 'Well, Walter, what about getting this van moved?'

'I need to get the fence fixed first,' he said.

'I've got some fencing timbers and I'll fetch 'em right away. Then I can drag the van out with my tractor...'

Satisfied that the two men were not going to come to blows over the incident, I explained I had an appointment in Ashfordly and left the scene. The van, in its present situation, was not causing a problem to other traffic and the two men were quite capable of recovering it without creating further hazards. I drove to Ashfordly Police Station because I was due to relieve Alf Ventress for an hour. I could complete my accident report whilst there.

'Thanks, Nick,' said Alf when I arrived. 'I'll be about an hour.'

'No problem, I've an accident report I can be getting on with,' I said, hanging up my cap and coat.

'Nothing too serious, I hope?' he asked.

'No, just a van which ran off the road trying to avoid a black dog.'

'A black dog? Not that same dog again, is it?'

'It could be, it's a black labrador by all accounts.'

'Not another accident! Around the sub-division, we've had dozens lately which have been attributed to a black dog running into the road,' he told me 'Have a look in the statistics file for the last six months, Nick. You'll see lots were caused by black dogs on the loose ... well, I must go. Can't keep my dentist waiting.'

It didn't take long to complete the accident report which I placed in the sergeant's in-tray and then I decided to check the stats. file as Alf had suggested. I was quite surprised to find that, out of nearly 800 traffic accidents within the sub-division in the preceding six months (most of which were minor ones) at least eighty were attributed to a dog suddenly running into the road.

The stats. file did not contain precise details of those accidents, but it was enough to make me ponder on the extent of the black dog's roamings. Just how far was it travelling? And why was it causing so many accidents without being caught? I wondered if any one had done deeper research into this phenomenon. It was the sort of thing which might be undertaken by the Accident Prevention Department at Force Headquarters. They maintained road maps of the entire county with the location of every accident recorded with coloured markers. A black stick-on dot about the size of a sixpence denoted a fatal accident, for example, and in that way, notorious accident locations could be identified. This was particularly evident when fatalities happened frequently at the same location, hence the term *accident black-spot*. A red dot marked a serious accident and in this way, road defects could be identified and eventually corrected. So would the department have mapped all the county's accidents involving black dogs? That thought made me wonder how long the dog had been at large – unless, of course, there was more than one!

A colleague from my initial training course, one of my friends, now worked in the Accident Prevention Department and so I decided, on the spur of the moment, to call him. One always got better service from a friend and I was pleased when he answered the phone.

'Accident Prevention, PC Cooper.'

'Hello, Malcolm, Nick Rhea speaking from Ashfordly.'

After a few moments of catching up with our respective news, I said, 'I'm ringing about accident stats., Malcolm. I've just completed a report involving a chap on my beat, and it prompted Alf Ventress to make a comment which set me thinking. I thought you might throw some light on it.'

'Well, yes, I'll do what I can. So what's the problem.'

'A black dog,' I responded.

He groaned loudly. 'Not another one, Nick! Go on, tell me about it.'

Wondering why he had groaned at my reference to a black dog, I provided a brief account of Alec Moore's accident and his explanation for it.

After listening patiently, Malcolm said, 'It's the good old black-dog syndrome. That's what we call it here in the office. You know there's no such thing, Nick? No black dog. Or, to be very precise, there isn't one which is causing all these accidents.'

'Isn't there? But we've dozens of road accidents in Ashfordly's books alone which blame a black dog running free.'

'Of course, Nick. What else can a driver blame if he does something stupid like running off the road in his car or on his bike? You'd be amazed how many cyclists coming home from the pub will blame a rogue black dog when they crash on sharp corners. That poor old black dog gets the blame for everything.'

'But you record those accidents, don't you? As part of your statistics?'

'We have to if a motorist or cyclist claims

the dog was the cause of their accident. That's the problem, Nick: no one can prove there was a black dog which was running loose on the road, but equally no one can prove there wasn't.'

'I can believe that! One man's word against another?'

'Exactly. So all I can say is that if that black dog is the cause of so many accidents around our county, he must cover a huge mileage in just a few hours. Or there are lots of black dogs at large, all running in front of cars and vans ... but I'll bet there's none reported missing. Did you check the missing dogs register?'

'As a matter of fact, I did, when I got my local accident report. And we've none reported missing in our area.'

'Well, there you are. I reckon that dog is a figment of your driver's imagination.'

'So it's all a myth? Like the Loch Ness Monster?'

'It is and we're perpetuating it. We've lots of stickers on our maps which blame black dogs for causing traffic accidents and so, officially, the dog exists. Along with its many colleagues, it's causing accidents all over England and Wales. And, Nick, you'd be amazed how many policemen blame black dogs if they have an accident while driving official vehicles on duty!'

'So how long has this being going on?' I asked out of curiosity.

'I'm not sure. I'd guess it's ever since man took to the roads in wheeled vehicles. In former times, when a stagecoach ran off the road or crashed without any good reason, the driver would claim a black dog had frightened the horses. I think our black dog dates to those times, except, of course, in days gone by, a black dog was thought to be the Devil in disguise.'

'I think it still is,' was all I could think of saying, wondering if experiencing a devil of a fright was a factor in modern accident statistics.

The most numerous of dogs on the moors and in the dales must surely be the black and white collie which is universally known simply as a sheepdog. Its formal name is Border collie, although many Yorkshire people refer to it as a cur, and in some areas it is called a bobtail collie. Many television viewers will recognize this dog from programmes such as *One Man and His Dog*, or from country shows where sheepdog trials feature as a competition, the dog being controlled by a series of whistles, shouts and sometimes hand movements as it herds flocks of sheep.

The cur is instantly recognizable due to its black and white coat, although some have tan patches. The body is mainly black with white underparts, usually with a white face and chest, but the pattern can vary from dog to dog. Most have smooth coats although long-haired varieties are not unusual, and in all cases their ears are pointed while turning over at the tips. They are highly intelligent animals who can be trained to undertake very complex tasks – one favourite demonstration is to separate a particular single sheep from a flock. Curs are especially skilled at rounding up stragglers which stray from the main flock, and one of their strengths is that they never bark at sheep and never touch them. One of their habits is to stare at sheep, almost as if hypnotizing them from what appears to be a crouching position, and that form of unwavering eye will invariably force even the most stubborn of sheep into heading in the direction required by the knowledgeable and determined dog.

Beyond doubt, these dogs are natural herders who have inherited the instinct from generations of their ancestors, and even untrained pups will play by herding other small creatures into a corner. I've seen them gather up ducks, geese and even pet rabbits and guinea pigs, naturally herding them into a secure place. This kind of thing is done instinctively to please the dog's master – it herds the animals towards him or towards a place where he can collect them. They can be trained though to take them away from their master too, in defiance of that instinct. Their skills are prominent in the countryside during the agricultural show season when they excel in trials or obedience tests, sometimes with young dogs working alongside as part of their tuition.

Every owner of curs is immensely proud of the dogs' prowess. Their skill and inventiveness while working is a constant topic of conversation in pubs or local markets, often with a small bet or challenge of some kind to fuel discussion, and those dogs which belong to expert trainers, especially when in the public eye, are often hotly debated in villages and on farms as the local chaps assert their dogs could do better. Some will argue that bitches are more skilful than dogs, so, the remarkable talents of sheepdogs provoke never-ending debate and deep pride.

During my time at Aidensfield, it was

necessary for the keeper of a dog which was more than six months old to obtain a licence from the post office or local authority offices. A licence cost 7s. 6d. (37.5p) and lasted twelve months from the first day of the month in which it was taken out. In addition, when on a highway or any place of public resort, every dog, even those under six months of age, had to wear a collar bearing the owner's name and address. However, there were exceptions to these rules.

Working dogs were not required to wear collars, and included in this were packs of hounds, or any dog being used for sporting purposes, or for the capture or destruction of vermin, or for driving or tending sheep or cattle. This was to avoid them getting their collars caught on protruding bits of hedges and fences which kind of accident could easily injure or perhaps kill a dog. Similarly, hounds under the age of twelve months belonging to a master of hounds and not entered in a pack did not need dog licences, neither did dogs used as guides by blind people. Furthermore, dogs kept solely for tending cattle or sheep did not require a dog licence, but this applied only if their owners had obtained a certificate of exemption from the local magistrates' court. The shepherd or farmer in question had to visit the magistrates' clerk in town and make a declaration before this exemption could be granted – and not surprisingly many did not bother to apply. I'm sure lots of sheepdog owners didn't bother with licences anyway! It was the latter exemption which prompted a farmer called Joe Jeffries to contact me.

'It's Jeffries from Manor Farm at Ploatby,' he shouted into my telephone one morning. 'Can you pop in when you're out this way to explain that business about sheepdogs not needing licences.'

'It's quite simple,' I said. 'I can tell you straight away. All you have to do is pop down to Eltering to the Magistrates' Clerk's office and fill in a form, then the court will approve your application. If a policeman asks for your dog licence, you should show him that bit of paper; it's called a certificate of exemption.'

'Aye, that's what I understand, but I still need to talk it over with you, Mr Rhea. I've a slight problem.'

'Fair enough. I'm heading for Ashfordly in about an hour's time, so I'll pop in on the way. Quarter past ten?'

'Aye, grand. See you then,' and the line went dead.

Manor Farm at Ploatby was a large and busy enterprise with both livestock and arable land, with dozens of outbuildings arranged protectively around the hilltop house. The spacious house was substantially built of local stone beneath a blue tiled roof and although the farm had earlier been owned by the local estate, it now belonged to Joe Jeffries. His father had bought it from the estate some years earlier and, as was the custom of this region, it had been handed down to his son. Joe, now in his mid-fifties, also had a son who would inherit the entire farm. When I arrived, I was welcomed by Mrs Jeffries – Jean – and taken into the huge kitchen where a plate of jam tarts and some coffee mugs were already waiting on the table.

'Sit yourself down, Mr Rhea, Joe'll be here in a tick, he's expecting you.'

I made myself comfortable as she fussed over making the coffee with hot milk and we chatted about the weather. Then Joe arrived. The back door opened and in bounded three Border collies, all rushing over to sniff at me and then heading for Jean who patted them as Joe commanded them to sit and behave themselves. They obeyed, sitting in a row like three wise monkeys with their tongues lolling out and their tails rapping the tiled floor, each awaiting Joe's next order as they sat with their eyes firmly fixed on him. I noticed he carefully avoided making eye contact with them as he sat at the table to enjoy his break. They had been told to sit and wait and so they would not move until he said so.

'Good of you to come at such short notice, Mr Rhea.' He was one of the older generation who was always formal with people in authority such as the doctor, vicar and policeman.

'No problem, Joe.' I used his forename which was expected of me. 'I was passing anyway. So how can I help you?'

'Well, I don't know whether it's owt to do with the police, but it's about these two dogs,' and he pointed at the two nearest to him, an action which set their tails wagging all over again and their legs twitching, as if they were preparing to dash off somewhere. 'Bob and Bess.'

At the sound of their names, each whimpered and wanted to get up but their training was such that they did not move.

'You said it was to do with sheepdogs not needing licences?' I tried to steer the conversation towards the matter in hand.

'You asked about the exemption certificate.'

'Aye, I did, but you see, these aren't my dogs, Mr Rhea. Those two, that is. I'm just looking after 'em for a week or two, mebbe longer.'

'How old are they? If they're under six months, they don't need licences anyway.'

'I'm not rightly sure how old they are, but looking at 'em, I'd say they were three months old. They're twins, by the way, a dog and a bitch.'

'So what's the story, Joe?'

Joe explained that Bob and Bess belonged to old Miss Lazenby who lived in Barn Owl Cottage near the bottom of the village. Everyone knew her, she was in her early eighties and everyone called her Henrietta. She'd acquired the two dogs from a distant relative, the idea being they would be both company for her because she was unable to get far from her house due to her age and lack of transport, and also a form of protection. What the relatives, and indeed Henrietta, had failed to realize was that sheepdogs need to work, and that their natural work is herding sheep. They are not house dogs or pets and even though these two dogs were very young when she'd acquired them, they had soon reached the stage where they required firm training in keeping with their instincts. Joe thought they'd come from a dogs' home.

Poor Henrietta was unable to provide the necessary kind of training and things had worsened when she had taken to her bed because her legs had failed. 'She's gone off her legs,' as Joe put it. 'She has folks popping in to see to her, friends, neighbours, the district nurse and so on, but there's no way she can see to these dogs. She'd just turn them out on a morning, though she kept 'em well fed. They were left to their own devices a lot of the time, and that's not good for them or anybody else, so I said I'd take 'em in. In fact I can do with another dog because old Jess is getting on a bit and I need a young 'un to train alongside her. But Henrietta won't give up these two; she's let me have them for a few weeks ... an indefinite period, she said, a sort of loan till she can see to 'em herself. Which is why I'm wondering about their licences, Mr Rhea, seeing I've got care of 'em.'

'Well.' I prepared to air my knowledge. 'It's the person who keeps a dog who must apply for a licence. That isn't necessarily the owner. So if these were domestic pets, you'd have to apply for a licence to keep them even if they were just on loan. But that applies only to dogs over six months of age. However, Joe, if you are a farmer who uses dogs for solely tending sheep or cattle, then you can apply to be exempt. All you have to do is pop into the Magistrates' Clerk's office in Eltering and fill in a form, then you won't need licences for any of these dogs.'

'But if Henrietta keeps 'em, she'll need licences once they get to six months of age?'

'Right, because she's not using them for tending sheep or cattle.'

'That all seems a bit daft to me; poor old Henrietta without much money must get licences for t'same dogs I can keep without any.'

'That's the way of the world, Joe. So if you go and apply for that certificate of exemption, you'll have to say you are using these extra dogs for tending your sheep and cattle.'

'You know what, Mr Rhea, it might be easier just to get licences for 'em; they're only a few bob each and it's easier getting down to our post office than driving all t'way into Eltering to queue up and fill forms in.'

'I'd agree, but it's your decision, Joe. So do you think these pups will make good sheep dogs?'

'There's no doubt about it, they're naturals. Did you hear about 'em when they got loose in Ashfordly?'

'No, I must admit I hadn't heard that! So what happened?'

Joe told me that a few weeks earlier, Henrietta had turned out her dogs for their morning run and apparently they had trotted across the fields behind Ploatby to find their way into Ashfordly, a distance of only a mile or so. There they had wandered around the town centre until they had found the ducks who live beside the beck which flows through the town. There were about a hundred ducks, all mallards both male and female and, acting instinctively, Bob and Bess had set about rounding them up. With all their inbred skills, they had herded the ducks on to the road beside the beck and had then driven them into the market-place where they brought their flock to rest near the memorial to an earlier Lord Ashfordly.

The dogs had then squatted on the ground to keep the ducks there, occasionally darting out to round up adventurous ducks who tried to make a break for freedom. How long they would have contained the ducks is not known, but fortuitously Joe had arrived in Ashfordly to visit the bank and he had put the dogs into his Landrover, allowing the puzzled ducks to waddle back to their stream.

'Then there was that business with Lord Ashfordly's deer,' grinned Joe. He told me of another occasion when Bob and Bess had gone on walkabout to finish up in the parkland of Ashfordly Hall where they'd rounded up Lord Ashfordly's herd of fallow deer. They had driven them into the corner of a field to lie watching them until they'd been discovered by one of the estate employees.

'Mind you,' continued Joe, now cheerfully recounting the exploits of Bob and Bess. 'I can't say I believe that yarn about them rounding up a busload of tourists, but a chap in the pub told me the dogs had gone into town on one of their outings and had found a crowd of old folks standing near Ashfordly Memorial in the market-place, waiting for their bus to collect them. They reckon that when the bus pulled in, the dogs herded those folks towards it, but I can't say I believe it. But they'll herd almost anything, Mr Rhea, which is why I don't mind looking after them for as long as Henrietta will let me.'

And so it was that Joe Jeffries became a

sort of foster parent for Henrietta's pair of sheepdogs, and he used them on his farm, training them alongside his own Jess until they were highly proficient in their herding skills. He took them daily to visit Henrietta who had recovered enough to venture into her garden or down to the shop.

She was still incapable of taking them for a walk or looking after such an active pair of dogs, and so Joe kept them, even if they never actually belonged to him. He trained them to operate as a pair and was soon entering them in sheepdog trials.

A few years later, when they won their first trophy, the Ringdale Cup, at Brantsford Agricultural Show, he presented it to Henrietta.

Only then did she say he could keep the dogs. She died six months later.

One of the vexing questions of the 1960s, as traffic was increasing on our roads and travelling at higher speeds, was whether domestic or farm animals on the roads should carry lights during the hours of darkness. The relevant legislation was The Road Transport Lighting Act of 1957 which reiterated the quaint old rule that during the hours of darkness every lamp on a vehicle must be kept properly trimmed, lighted and in a clean and efficient condition. The basic rule was that any vehicle on a road during the hours of darkness must show a white light to the front and a red light to the rear. I have often wondered how one kept one's car lamps trimmed and I believe this word appeared in the regulations until 1989 when the Road Vehicles Lighting Regulations of that year introduced words such as dim-dip lighting device, running lamp, dipped beam headlamp, main beam headlamp, hazard warning signal device, side marker lamp, stop lamp, end-outline marker lamp and side retro reflector, the wicks of which did not require trimming.

The lighting laws, however, related only to vehicles, not only those which were motorized but also to pedal cycles and contraptions drawn by hand or by animals. I think it is fair to say that some horse-drawn vehicles, even in the 1960s, carried oil lamps which meant the old law of keeping them trimmed was quite valid. A trimmed wick gave a better light and I recall an old police pedal cycle which was still fitted with an acetylene lamp. I've no doubt the Sergeant Blaketons of the police service made sure its wick was always kept trimmed.

But none of the lighting regulations appeared to accommodate horses or dogs which might use our roads during the hours of darkness. One could dress in all-black clothing and legally take a black dog for a walk at night, however dangerous that might be to the dog, to oneself, or to other users of the road. Similarly, one could ride a black horse along the darkest of unlit rural lanes and although sensible riders carried lights on their horses, there was no legal obligation to do so. If we encountered a horse rider or dog walker at night without any kind of lighting to alert others to their presence, we would halt them to give what became known as 'suitable advice'. That could be anything from genuine advice to an almighty telling off.

But how does one cope with a dog which is riding a horse at night without any kind of lighting?

That might sound an odd sort of dilemma, but late one October evening, I was on foot patrol between Aidensfield and Maddleskirk when I heard the distinctive clip-clop sound of an approaching horse. I was walking in complete darkness in my dark police uniform but I was carrying a torch which, at that moment, was not illuminated. I was heading for Aidensfield and walking on the right of the narrow lane so as to face any oncoming traffic; there was none, however, and I was on my way home after an evening foot patrol.

My eyes were accustomed to the darkness and soon I could distinguish the silhouette of the oncoming horse; the distant skyline made it visible to me and the horse did not appear to have a rider. So, was someone walking beside it? It was still some distance away and I did not like to shine my torch directly at it in case the light startled the animal. As it drew closer, I could see it more clearly and then, without a word of command from anyone, it halted at my side. I switched on my torch, making sure the light shone down to the road surface instead of in the horse's eyes, and now I could see it in greater detail.

It was a handsome Cleveland Bay in dark tan with a black mane and tail, and it was carrying a saddle and reins which were knotted and hanging loose at the horse's shoulders, albeit not reaching the ground. But standing firmly on the saddle with legs apart was a small Jack Russell terrier. And that was all. No one else was accompanying the horse. The little dog was in sole charge.

As I approached, the dog wagged its tail and the horse shook its head. I wondered if the horse had enough intelligence to realize it should not be walking on the road at night with only a tiny dog in charge. Maybe that was why it halted when it discovered my presence? I was somewhat flustered by this dilemma for I felt sure the horse and dog had wandered away from their owner. Surely, this daring evening stroll was not a regular event? As I wondered what to do next, I remembered that the daughter of the farmer who lived in Abbey Farm, Aidensfield, was a keen rider with several horses in her stable.

From my place on that road, this was the nearest house and it seemed sensible to take the horse there, if only to remove it from the highway where I felt it was a source of danger to traffic.

I spoke to it, and to the dog, took the rein near the horse's head and it turned and followed me without any kind of protest. I decided to leave the dog on board; it seemed very capable of maintaining its balance on the saddle. I had only covered about quarter of a mile when I saw the headlamp of a pedal cycle heading towards me, and soon I could hear the heavy panting of its rider as she tried to coax more speed from her machine. I flashed my torch so she would see me and my companions, and so she eased to a halt at my side. It was Jenny Hopper from Abbey Farm, a pretty young woman about twenty-two years old, daughter of the owner.

'Oh, there you are, you naughty dog ... sorry, Mr Rhea, but they shouldn't be out like this.'

'I must admit I wondered if they had run away together...'

'No, we were in the foldyard and I had to rush in to answer the telephone and the gate must have been open. Gip likes riding, he'll usually stand behind me, on the horse's back, or if I'm with two horses, he'll ride bareback on the second one. Thanks for finding them and bringing them home.'

She turned her bike around and walked beside me. I told her I would hold the horse's bridle until we reached Abbey Farm which meant she could concentrate on wheeling her bicycle, but Gip the terrier remained in the saddle. During that short walk, I discovered that Gip had been introduced to horse riding as a tiny pup when he was small enough to be carried in the pocket of a riding jacket; as he'd grown bigger, he'd been allowed to stand on the horse and so he'd grown up

215

thinking all Jack Russell terriers rode horses. I wondered how far the pair might have travelled had I not met them. I didn't, though, inform the sergeant I had dealt with a dog which was riding a horse without lights during the hours of darkness.

Chapter 8

What is not generally appreciated by out-siders is that the district around Aidensfield and Ashfordly contains many thatched cot-tages. In the past, the simple homes of moor folk were thatched with ling, i.e. heather, but now the preferred materials are either reeds or straw. Fortunately, skilled thatchers are still active which means the houses are well maintained. Today, of course, they are not the homes of the poor and lowly. Instead, they suggest wealth and style, with nice examples being seen in places such as Farndale, Rievaulx, Harome, Beadlam, Pockley, Scackleton, Old Malton, Thornton-le-Dale and even on the coast at Runswick Bay or in the suburbs of Scarborough.

There is a fine example in the grounds of

Ryedale Folk Museum at Hutton-le-Hole, and among Yorkshire's thatched inns are the Crab and Lobster at Asenby near Thirsk, and the Star Inn at Harome near Helmsley. Perhaps the best known thatched dwelling house in North Yorkshire is Beck Isle Cottage at Thornton-le-Dale near Pickering which features regularly on postcards, Christmas cards, calendars and chocolate boxes. In addition to our thatched cottages, there used to be lots of other buildings with thatched roofs. They included cow byres, blacksmiths' shops, lychgates, summer houses, outbuildings of various kinds and even small structures like beehives, dovecots and outdoor toilets.

Before the revival of interest in this kind of roofing material, a high percentage of thatched roofs were replaced with tiles, and, unfortunately, some were covered with sheets of corrugated iron and wire netting. Ostensibly those tin coverings were to keep out mice and birds, and they were also a means of not having to periodically renew the thatch, but they made the houses look dreadful. That kind of reverse cosmetic treatment resulted in some very ugly cottages around the dales and on the moors, hardly in keeping with the handsome buildings which surrounded them. It was probably in the late 1980s that purchasers began to remove those iron roofs in favour of returning the buildings to their former picturesque thatch. Even today a thatched roof is a bonus – apart from its pleasing appearance, it keeps the building warm in winter and cool in summer, while modern developments help to reduce the fire risk and deter vermin infestation.

In my time at Aidensfield, a couple from Middlesbrough purchased one of those old iron-roofed cottages at Briggsby on my beat, knowing there was thatch beneath the tin lid. It was their ambition to restore the building to its former beauty and modernize it without detracting from any historical importance. They set about the work themselves, learning how to thatch and update the rest of the old house while living nearby in rented accommodation. The work was to be done mainly at weekends, although some evenings would necessarily be utilized, and they managed to acquire practical help from craftsmen and tradespeople in the village.

The couple were Robert and Louise Marshall. Robert, in his early forties, was a freelance photographer who worked for several local newspapers and magazines. He specialized in landscape photography, but also photographed weddings and other family events as a means of earning a fairly regular income.

Not surprisingly, he intended to photograph every stage of his renovation of Rose Cottage as a personal record of his endeavours. His wife, Louise, was a ladies' hairdresser who attended customers in their own homes, so the couple had the flexibility of the self-employed as they set about this massive task. An added factor was that they had no children – their time was their own.

In my capacity as village constable, I became aware of this project and met the couple on occasions while they were working. Rose Cottage was empty, so I promised to keep an eye on the premises during their regular absences which meant I could observe the changes as work progressed. First was the stripping of the dreadful corrugated iron sheets and the wire netting which enclosed the edges of the thatch. Underneath it all, the existing straw had rotted and was dank and black, the result of having a restricted circulation of air. With the iron sheets out of the way, the next job was to strip away all that filthy wet straw and dispose of it.

My visits to Briggsby were often in the course of what we called a route. That was a pre-determined tour, arranged by Divisional Headquarters, during which we patrolled for four hours, visiting nominated places each hour. Those four hours might be in the early morning, during the day or late at night. Without any particular reason for a visit, I called at remote places like Briggsby once in a while. It meant I could spend time in the village preventing crime, showing the uniform or being available for consultation. One of the chores was to stand for five minutes at a given time at the local telephone kiosk in case I was required by the office for anyhing, even though I had a police radio in my vehicle.

One Saturday morning in early May, I was standing at Briggsby telephone kiosk for my allotted five minutes when I noticed Robert Marshall striding towards me.

'Ah, Mr Rhea, glad I caught you. I've a little problem which I think is a police matter.'

'You've not found a skeleton buried in that cottage of yours, I hope!' That was quite a regular occurrence for people renovating old houses. Some old buildings had been placed over ancient burial grounds, consequently such a find was not too unusual, but he shook his head.

'No, I think it's a hoard of silver cutlery. Quite a lot of it. We found it yesterday. It's black with age, or perhaps discolouration, so I'm not sure whether it is real silver. Don't I have to report it as treasure trove? I once photographed a hoard of coins found under the floorboards of an old house and remember the coroner had to be involved.'

'If it's silver, yes. Finds like that are only considered to be treasure trove if it's silver or gold, or if it contains any silver or gold. Any other valuable things like jewellery or historic artefacts can't be treasure trove. And to qualify as treasure trove, it has to be deliberately hidden, not just lost or abandoned.'

'Well, this lot was in the roof. I've no idea how long it's been there, but clearly it didn't get there by accident. It's been pushed deep into the straw, Mr Rhea, piece by piece, and there's a lot of it. I'm not talking of just a spoon or a knife, it looks like a full set, or even more.'

'I'd better have a look at it.' So I followed him to Rose Cottage where Louise was in the kitchen with the cutlery in the sink. At that time there was no hot water in the house, other than a kettle they'd brought

221

with them, but she had boiled it and was trying to wash the grime away from the cutlery. She was being very careful because she did not want to damage the items, but from a glance, it looked just like an assortment of very dirty and cheap knives, forks and spoons.

'I think it's silver,' she said. 'I'm sure there are hallmarks on all these, and they've all got the same shell pattern on the handles. But it's not a single full set because there's a different number of knives and forks. I've counted forty forks but only two dozen knives, and there's dozens of spoons, large and small. I think they've been pushed under our thatch at different times.'

She passed one of the cleanest of the forks to me and I took it across to the light from the tiny window. Certainly it was almost completely black but the embossed shell pattern was quite clear on the handle, and on the other side was what seemed to be a hallmark. I was not sufficiently knowledgeable to be able to interpret the hallmark, but I knew that, to an expert, it would reveal the date and place of manufacture, and even the name of the maker.

'Louise, can we offer Mr Rhea a cup of coffee? We've got to get this business sorted out before we go any further.'

'Thanks,' I said. 'And while we're enjoying that, I'll explain the procedure.'

As the coffee was being prepared, Robert led me outside to look at the place where the cutlery had been hidden. The eaves were very low, easily reached by a person of average height without a ladder, and he showed me a section of the roof, now devoid of thatch and bare down to the laths which formed the inner lining. It was close to the front entrance, near the rise of the roof which covered the front porch. The front porch overlooked the village street, albeit set well back from the road, but in days gone by, without street lighting, that corner would be dark and sheltered yet close to the house entrance. I guessed it would be considered ideal for concealing things whilst making them reasonably accessible.

He patted the space and said, 'Right here, tucked under the thatch. The stuff had been pushed deep, a good two feet into the thatch, and the cutlery was not all in one place. It's almost as if it was thrust in there over a long period, item by item. It wasn't in a box or container of any kind. We almost threw it out with the straw, but once we realized it was there, we sifted the straw as we disposed of it and kept finding more pieces. I think we've got it all now I've taken photographs, by the way, right from our first discovery and as we found more, and I've got a picture of the whole lot in its dirty condition. I'll take more when we get the things cleaned up.'

'That could be useful for the inquest,' I said. 'Let me see them when you've got them developed.'

We returned to the kitchen where Louise had produced some chocolate biscuits and mugs of coffee, and I sat down to explain the procedure. I told them that the first task was to establish whether or not these items were made of silver. If they were, the law of treasure trove would become effective. If not, the cutlery would belong to the Marshalls, unless there was some other legitimate claimant. I said it might be wise to trace previous occupants or their descendants to check whether anything was known of this hoard.

'We've found quite a lot of that history already,' said Robert. 'Some of it is from a local history book and some from the deeds, but the house was owned by the Briggsby Estate until the estate was sold in 1947, just after the war. Until then, the occupants of this cottage were estate workers, labourers, maids and such. Hardly the sort to own a silver cutlery service! Since then, it's had only one lot of occupants, an old couple. They died a few years ago and their relations kept the old house empty until we bought it. They know nothing about the hoard – I telephoned them last night. Certainly, the cutlery didn't belong to that old couple, the family is sure about that, so it must have been in the thatch all the time they were living here.'

'Fair enough. It's important you can show you've done all in your power to trace the true owners. There's no doubt in my mind it was hidden there for reasons we don't know, but if the stuff is silver, or has silver in it such as the handles of the knives, I must inform the coroner.'

'Does that mean we lose it all?' asked Louise.

'Yes and no,' I said. 'He will hold an inquest, that's an enquiry into the circumstances of the concealment of the cutlery. If he is satisfied it is silver and that it was deliberately hidden, he will declare it treasure trove. That means it must be handed to the Crown, which in reality means it goes into the British Museum, and you will be paid the full market value. It will be valued by an independent assessor.'

'Oh, well, that seems all right. And if it's not treasure trove, does he decide who then owns it?'

'No, that's not his job. If it is not treasure trove, it's a matter for the finder to sort out. That's not usually difficult unless somebody else comes forward to make a claim. You seem to have removed that possibility. And in this case, it's abundantly clear the stuff was hidden, no one could accidentally lose it up there in the roof! So it looks as though you've got treasure trove on your hands, and it might prove valuable. You've done the right thing in declaring it.'

'So do you take it away?'

'Yes, but I'll give you a detailed receipt.'

'Thanks. I'd rather you kept it in safe custody, Mr Rhea; I wouldn't feel happy having it under my roof, if you pardon the expression, especially if it's valuable.'

I explained that the inquest would normally be completed within three months, the coroner waiting until he had several treasure-trove cases to consider at the same sitting. When I counted all those items, there were thirty-eight spoons, forty forks, eighteen teaspoons, a butter knife, four salt spoons, twelve table knives and twelve dessert knives. Robert took more photographs, some of the whole set and some individual items. Although they were now clean, with years of dirt having been carefully washed away, we decided not to attempt to polish them. Each of us felt they should be examined in their existing black condition by an expert who might then advise the best way to clean or care for them. We found a box to accommodate them, I gave the Marshalls my receipt, and said I would be in touch when I had more news.

My first task was to decide whether these items were made of silver, and for that I would consult a silversmith in Ashfordly. To cut short a long story, the cutlery was all made of silver and it was hallmarked, but there were several dates of manufacture, namely 1817, 1841 and 1845. It was known as a shell service, but clearly, due to the different dates, the pieces had been made at different times, thus it was not a single set. The silversmith expressed his opinion that it had all the appearance of having been collected piece by piece over several years, but he could not hazard a guess as to why it had been hidden in such a strange way.

I compiled my report for the coroner who confirmed he would hold an inquest and I would be notified of the date in due course. Meanwhile, the cutlery was lodged in Ashfordly Police Station safe. I drove out to Briggsby to inform the Marshalls.

'You know what I think, Mr Rhea?' said Robert when I called. 'I think whoever lived in this cottage worked at the big house, and was stealing those bits and pieces over the years. And hiding them in the thatch. Out of spite, perhaps? Jealous of the wealth of the lord and master? A maid taking the odd piece every so often? Not really wanting to build a complete service because the owner would miss the pieces if they all disappeared, but stealing a knife here, a fork there and spoons when the fancy took her. The pieces would probably be considered lost and perhaps never missed by the owners. That makes sense to me. Does the coroner go into that kind of detail?'

'No, he'll just make a decision as to whether it was hidden deliberately; he won't try to research into the history or anything like that. And if it was stolen from the big house all those years ago, we'll never know, will we? There'll be no records now and there's no one to make a formal complaint. Besides, we'd never get the stuff formally identified as coming from the manor, so we can forget any criminal action.'

'Won't the descendants of Lord Briggsby still have bits of that service? They might know that some went missing years ago...'

'It's always possible, but that's a hurdle we'll have to cross if and when it arises.' I tried to reassure Robert that he was worrying needlessly. 'There might be publicity in which case someone might come forward, but establishing a claim would be a job for the civil courts, not for me, or the coroner.'

Robert was now able to give me a set of photographic prints which I would include with the official file and in due course, HM Coroner ruled that the hoard of cutlery was treasure trove. In accordance with the law, it was handed over to the British Museum who paid the sum of £3,500 to the Marshalls, that being an independent assessment of the cutlery's value. The highly useful bonus, a large sum of money at that time, went towards making their little home one of the finest thatched cottages in the district.

From time to time I wondered if Robert had actually discovered a hoard of goods which had been systematically stolen and hidden more than a century earlier. If that was the case, it hadn't been of much benefit to the thief, whoever he or she was. And to my knowledge, no one ever came forward to make a claim or provide a better explanation for their curious concealment.

It is well known that people tend to hide things which are important or valuable, or which have great sentimental importance. Each of us can boast our own special place for concealing precious things, but there are occasions when this squirrel-like tendency emulates the less welcome aspects of wild life.

In other words, a grey squirrel (who does not hibernate) will hide hazelnuts in the autumn so that there is a regular supply of food in the winter months, but then it will forget where they are hidden. A squirrel's memory is not good enough to remind it of the whereabouts of that hoard, and so a search will follow. The only way the squirrel will trace that hoard is by smell – and if some other thing has obliterated the hiding place or stolen the nuts, the squirrel will remain hungry for a while longer. In due course, if not found, its hoard of nuts will probably sprout to produce some valuable young trees – it's all part of nature's grand plan.

The drawbacks of the squirrels' system also affect human beings because a person will conceal something very precious by hiding it in a wonderfully cunning place, only to later forget where it is. People such as auctioneers or house-clearers, or even house buyers, will often find money or other precious things which have been hidden in desks, drawers or wardrobes, sometimes in specially constructed secret compartments. The past owner of an object may have died or moved away, or even forgotten all about it which means he or she will not benefit from that earlier care.

The snag with hiding things about the house is that while we all believe we have discovered the most perfect place for safe concealment, the fact is we all tend to think alike and choose almost identical places. Burglars know this only too well, so there are very few places which are totally secure or original. Almost every type of hiding place within the home has been previously used by someone, but that does not deter those squirrel-like people as they continue their habit.

Such a person was old Mrs Nancy Knott, a widow who lived in the aptly named Hazel Cottage in Elsinby. Not surprisingly, her nickname was Nutty Knott. Everyone referred to her as Nutty, not with any malice because she knew that was her name and often referred to it herself. Well into her eighties, she was a tiny lady who trotted about the village, often helping those less capable than herself by doing bits of shopping or posting letters, and she habitually wore a heavy fur stole with a fox's head at one end. But Mrs Knott, like the squirrel, frequently concealed things about her house and then forgot where she'd put them.

If I happened to be in the village while she was hunting for some lost treasure, she would ask for my help and sometimes I would produce the answer. I based this on the knowledge that old folks all tend to select similar hiding places and so, if she couldn't find the insurance man's money which she'd put aside for him, I would say, 'Have you looked under the plant pot?' or 'Is it under that stone outside the back door?' or 'Did you leave it on the window ledge of the outside toilet?' Or even 'Are you sure he hasn't been to collect it?' Nutty Knott had certain places she used regularly so it wasn't difficult to find what she sought. Friends, neighbours and local tradesmen would all join in these searches which meant, of course, that nothing was ever truly concealed by Mrs Knott. Almost everyone in Elsinby knew her secret hiding places. Nonetheless, she persisted in her habit, probably the entire village population at some point having helped her to find things. The only people who never found anything were burglars and thieves, simply because they never paid her a visit.

Because she was a widow, Mrs Knott would often go away for the weekend to visit her only son, Gerald, the eldest of her four children; the other girls lived some distance away. All came to visit her when they could, but Gerald was headmaster of a private school near Harrogate and quite regularly on a Friday evening would drive over to Elsinby to collect his mother for the weekend, then return her on the Sunday evening. He was quite well known in Elsinby having lived there as a child and young man. Often, he found himself searching Nutty's house before leaving on Fridays because she'd hidden the front door key somewhere, or placed her money somewhere safe ready for the weekend. He once found her cash hidden in a pile of newspapers, and accidentally discovered her will behind a painting hanging on her bedroom wall. Among the most puzzling of incidents was when she hid

£20 in £1 notes in the hem of the curtains in the lounge, put her wedding ring in the sugar basin, placed a bag of saved sixpences in a sack of potatoes in her garden shed, and left her back-door key under the compost bin.

Her behaviour at the time of the concealments seemed perfectly logical to Mrs Knott even if she couldn't remember why she had done so when asked later. Eventually Mrs Knott died of old age and was buried in Elsinby churchyard. Her immediate family and lots of relations turned up for the funeral and afterwards joined her friends from the village in the Hopbind Inn. It was a good farewell for a very nice old lady who would undoubtedly be missed, especially by those who'd spent hours in her house looking for things she had hidden.

Afterwards, Gerald and his sisters had the task of clearing her small house and disposing of the contents before putting the property on the market. On Monday during the half-term holidays, I saw his car outside and later came across him in the Hopbind Inn where he was having a sandwich and pint as a break from his chores. He was working alone that day. I had popped into the pub, in uniform, as part of my daily duty, not to have a drink but simply to keep in touch with events in the village. One often picked up good crime-busting information in a pub!

'Hello, Nick,' Gerald was an affable character. 'Can I get you one?'

'Sorry, Gerald, not while I'm on duty. I'm sure I'll catch you one of these days when I'm socializing!'

'I just wanted to say thanks for all you did for Mother before she died. I know you spent time, like we all did, looking for things she'd hidden.'

'It was nothing.' I shrugged my shoulders. 'I was just glad to help her now and again, like all the villagers did.'

'I'm clearing the house. I've got a team of professional clearers coming in next week, and we'll be selling the stuff at auction before the house goes on the market, but I'm here to go through everything in case she'd hidden anything! I know she's hidden her jewellery, for example, so I'll have to look into every conceivable hiding place. Maybe I should get your chaps in? They're pretty good at searching premises, I believe!'

'Or a professional burglar who's going straight!' I suggested. 'But seriously, if you need help, don't be frightened to ask. I might be able to suggest one or two unlikely hiding places. Like the toilet cistern, or inside the back of the television.'

'Thanks, I'll try there. She must have put it somewhere.'

'You might have to take things to pieces,' I said. 'I know one old character who built a false back to each of the drawers in the chest in his bedroom, and each was stuffed with cash in notes. Thousands of pounds...'

He groaned. 'I don't think she'd resort to carpentry like that, but really she was good at hiding things, too good if I'm honest.'

And so I left. By the end of the week, Gerald was still at his mother's house during the day, still searching the furniture and fittings for things she might have left behind, and I encountered him again in the Hopbind Inn. He was having his Friday lunch when I arrived, once more on duty. The landlord, George Ward, was behind the bar and we were the only people in at that moment. There was the usual chat about the weather and village events, and then Gerald said, 'Nick, I'm at my wits' end! Just you ask George!'

'Why?'

'I've searched every inch of Mother's house and been through all her belongings, clothes, furniture, fittings, the lot and although I've found all sorts of things like cash and lots of cheap trinkets, I can't find any jewellery. And that's what I'm looking for now. I don't relish the idea of selling up without finding it as somebody else might well come across it, but I don't know where to look next.'

George and myself then gave the benefit of our wisdom by suggesting all manner of odd places, but Gerald assured us he had checked them all. In fact, he'd invited several people in from the village to help, men and women who'd helped his mother on previous occasions. They'd double-checked every item of household goods from the tea caddy to the three-piece suite, including bed-linen in the airing cupboard and every piece of clothing or curtaining. They found a few items but not the jewellery. They'd checked every inch of the house too, including the loft and outbuildings, again without finding what they sought.

'Are you sure she's hidden the jewellery?' I asked.

'Yes, it's in her will. She says she has hidden the jewellery in the house and I must find it and share it out with my sisters and myself. There's all sorts – a few necklaces, several rings, bracelets, earrings, brooches, some with diamonds in or embossed with gold or silver; there's pearls too ... she had quite a collection which she'd amassed over the years. I think it's quite valuable. I didn't see any lying around in recent weeks.'

'Because she'd hidden it?' I asked.

'So it would seem. So, Nick, as a police-man, where do you think an old lady would hide her most valuable possessions?'

Other than the possible places I'd already mentioned, I had no idea. I pointed out that each item in itself was rather small, so indivi-dually they wouldn't take up a lot of space. A diamond ring, for example, could be easily concealed in the lining of a coat, the hem of a skirt, or even behind a piece of loose wall-paper, whilst something like a pearl necklace could easily be lost among Christmas-tree decorations, or pushed into hollow bedposts. If she had concealed the pieces item by item, they could be lurking anywhere. Collectively, he told me, her jewellery might fill a small drawer or even something the size of a small shoebox, but he'd checked all those likely places. He added he had carefully checked every tiniest place for objects as small as rings, all without success.

'I can't spend much longer on this,' he told

me. 'We're due back at school next week so my time's very limited. My sisters and their husbands have helped as well, but all we want now is to sell the house as soon as we can; we don't want it standing empty for too long, and of course, the furnishings must go soon. It's infuriating, knowing the stuff is somewhere in there but not being able to find it. I've no idea what her jewellery is worth either, so it's not the money, it's just the fact it's here and we can't find it.'

'Now you know how the police feel when we know someone's guilty but can't prove it!'

'*Touché!* But you've given me an idea, Nick. What about the police searching my house? As an exercise, I mean. Surely drugs officers and detectives are taught how to search premises in the greatest detail, so could they come and practice here? I'd willingly let them into the house for as long as it takes. They could even dig up the floor-boards if it was necessary.'

'It would be a good exercise, but I doubt the chief constable would allow his men to do that sort of thing. I can always ask, but I think your best bet is to ask a friendly detective to come in his spare time, as a favour to you...'

'How about you then? You could help me as a friend; we've known each other long enough.'

'I don't mind giving you any kind of help, I can even pop in now and look at the place, just to give you pointers in case you've overlooked anywhere, but I couldn't do it as a professional search, if you understand the distinction.'

'I do; I was joking really, flying kites, but it shows how desperate I am.'

'All right, I'll come in now and see if I can find a place you've overlooked.'

I spent about three-quarters of an hour touring the small house with Gerald, pointing at places I thought he might have overlooked, such as the loft or under the floor boards, up the chimneys, in the toilet cisterns, in false drawers, tucked into curtain hems or wrapped up in clothes and blankets, under the mattress, under the carpet, in her own clothes, in tins of other things ranging from tea caddies to tins of buttons, tucked between pages of books or in hollowed-out novels. I knew a man who hid his gold watch each night in a deep hole he had cut in the pages of a book.

For every place I mentioned, though, Gerald told me that he and others had searched there, even to the extent of running their fingers along the hems of blankets and sheets to see if anything was hidden within them. I could see he was really frustrated about his lack of success, but felt there was little else I could do. As a final gesture of interest, I asked if he had a copy of the will with him, just in case he had misunderstood his mother's wishes. He produced it from his briefcase and allowed me to read the relevant section. It seemed very clear, saying, 'I leave all my jewellery to my son Gerald and my daughters Ruth, Elaine and Penelope, to be equally distributed between them. I have hidden my jewellery for Gerald to find after my death.'

It was a simple instruction, written a year or so before Mrs Knott's death and it had clearly been agreed by her solicitor. Gerald had spoken to the solicitor during his current search, but was told his mother had not elaborated upon that clause when she'd spoken to him. It seemed so blindingly simple that I wondered if we had overlooked something. Time was pressing so I had to return the will to Gerald and tell him I must leave because I had an appointment in Thackerston. I left him to his own devices and wondered whether he would ever find his mother's jewellery.

That evening I was not on duty and Mary had arranged for Mrs Quarry to come and baby-sit for our brood of four children. We decided to pop down to the Hopbind Inn at Elsinby for a meal and a drink or two. It was within walking distance and the evening was fresh and mild, so we did not have to worry about drink/driving.

We arrived shortly after 7.30, had ordered our meal and settled in a cosy corner near the fire when I spotted Gerald Knott. He was alone and I called out to him, 'What are you having, Gerald? I'm buying.'

'Mine's a pint, Nick. Thanks, I need it!'

'Come and join us,' I invited.

Gerald joined Mary and I, our meals arriving at the same time thanks to the courtesy of George Ward's intervention with the kitchen staff. I introduced Mary who'd not met Gerald before. I had not discussed his dilemma with her; I tended not to discuss police work with anyone although I knew Mary was the soul of discretion, so I allowed Gerald to re-tell his tale of woe for her benefit. He explained his problem with more than a hint of humour, even if it was to disguise his real anxiety and afterwards Mary said, 'So you've still not found her jewellery, after all that searching?'

'Not a sausage,' said Gerald. 'We've searched the whole house, practically stripping it to the bare stones. And we've looked in everything that's inside the house.'

'Are you sure it's in her house?' asked Mary with all the innocence of someone taking a completely different perspective.

'Well, we've looked outside as well, the garden shed, the outside toilet, other likely outside places.'

'No, I meant are you certain she means her house?'

Gerald frowned. 'Well, yes. Where else might she have put it? She's been hiding things in her house all her life, as your husband and most of the villagers know.'

'What was the precise wording in the will?' I asked Gerald.

'You saw it, Nick. It said "I have hidden my jewellery for Gerald to find after my death". Those are her exact words.'

'Yes,' said Mary. 'But that doesn't mention her house, does it? And she expects you to find the stuff, she doesn't mention your sisters finding it even though they are beneficiaries. If it had been hidden in her own house, surely she'd have wanted any member of the family to find it, not just you?'

'So where else could she have put it?' he almost demanded.

'Your house,' smiled Mary. 'Didn't she often go there for weekends?'

Gerald said nothing for a long, long time and I could see that a sense of disbelief was creeping over his features. He was clearly running through some events in his mind and then he said, 'You know you could be right ... she came to us regularly, always used the same room. We've a Victorian wardrobe in there, one I got from an antique shop in Harrogate, and it's got a secret drawer in the base ... I showed it to Mother some time ago. I wonder if she's put her stuff in there? Smuggled it into *my* house in her suitcase...? Mary, you might have saved my sanity – and made me look something of a twit!'

'Woman's intuition!' was all I could think of saying.

'I've got to ring home,' said Gerald. 'I must find out before I leave here.'

Without waiting to finish his meal, he went to the public telephone at the end of the bar, but George saw him and realized his call might be rather more personal than calling a taxi so invited him to use the private phone. 'It'll save you feeding it with money,' he smiled. 'And you won't get cut off if your money runs out! Go through to our private quarters, it's on a shelf near the front door.'

From the domestic area of the pub, Gerald rang his wife, Sylvia, and explained his theory. She said she would go upstairs and look in the old wardrobe, then call back to save Gerald running up a hefty bill. Gerald waited and within five minutes, Sylvia returned his call. He rejoined us with his face showing a mixture of disbelief, anger and relief.

'The cunning old thing!' he said, picking up his glass and drinking deeply. 'Yes, it's there, Mary. All her jewellery is wrapped up in tissue paper and packed into empty flour bags. It's been in my house all the time ... and she never said a dicky bird...'

'I wonder what else she's hidden in your house?' I grinned mischievously. 'You'll have to start hunting all over again!'

'I think I'll leave that to my own children,' he said. 'So, how about another drink? I think we deserve a bottle of champagne after this, you especially, Mary.'

And so we had a lovely party before facing the daunting task of walking home. I hoped I was not called out during the night.

A few weeks later, after completion of the sale of Hazel Cottage and its contents, there was a knock on our front door.

When Mary answered, it was Gerald and his wife. They declined to come in as they were heading off to Scarborough, but Gerald gave Mary a small box. She opened it and there was a gold ring inside.

'The family wanted you to have this,' he said. 'You made us all very happy. Heaven knows how long we'd have taken to find mother's jewellery if you hadn't had that flash of inspiration.'

And to this day, Mary still wears Mrs Knott's signet ring.

Chapter 9

Aidensfield pound was on the edge of the village, a few yards across the moor at the junction which led to Eltering via one route and Ghylldale via another. It was a circular construction of local stone, built in the manner of a dry-stone wall with a stout metal gate secured by an equally stout lock. Its walls were about eight feet high and its internal area was roughly the size of half a tennis court.

Responsibility for its maintenance was one of the tasks of the parish council, but over the years, the pound had become rather neglected because it was very rarely used. Indeed, some neighbouring villages had restyled their pounds, turning them into peaceful gardens with park benches so that people could sit in peace and quiet to enjoy the sunshine. However, that had not yet happened to the Aidensfield pound. It remained very much an official feature of the village in the care of the parish council and as such liable to be used at any time.

In the past, the job of looking after a pound, otherwise known as a pinfold, was that of the pinder. He – and in most cases it was a man – was appointed by the parish council specifically to care for the pound and any of its inhabitants. Its purpose was to temporarily house animals which were found straying on the highway when their owner was not known, so it had to be strong enough and large enough to cater for, say, horses, cattle, donkeys, pigs, sheep or indeed any other farm or domestic animal. It was the pinder's job to recover from the animals' owners any fees imposed for keeping them, and any costs involved in feeding them while there. Income from pound fees was a source of income for the parish.

If the pound fees were not paid by the animals' owner within three days, the creatures could later be sold, provided seven days' notice of that intention was given to the owner. The pinder, of course, would only release the animals when the necessary fees and costs had been paid, and if any owner tried to release his animals without authority and without paying the fees, he was guilty of an offence known as pound breach. It follows that both the pound and the pinder were of some importance in a village, albeit with the pinder sometimes not being the most popular of officials.

In the case of Aidensfield, moorland sheep roamed freely around the village and on its spacious green, so they were not subjected to the normal rules of straying animals; they enjoyed ancient rights of free grazing even if they did wander across the roads. But if cattle, horses and other livestock took it into their heads to go walkabout in or around the village, they could be impounded. In areas where there was no pound, animals found straying would be returned to their owners' field if known, or driven into any other suitable place, e.g. a paddock or compound. However, there was danger in this. If a diseased or dangerous animal was driven into a field which was home to others, it could cause untold harm or damage, so the village pound was invaluable. One of the lessons to be learned when visiting the countryside is that well-meaning people should not drive straying animals into a field unless they know beyond doubt that the field in question is their normal home.

The man who looked after Aidensfield's pound was a retired clerical worker who had formerly worked in County Hall at Northallerton.

His name was Hubert Braithwaite, a widower of about seventy years of age. Although he was not the official pinder, that post having been abolished many years earlier, he described himself as the pinder and had taken it upon himself to keep the pound in a clean and tidy condition, clearing away the rubbish that was sometimes thrown into it, cutting the grass inside and making sure the gate was locked to deter youngsters with bicycles or footballs. He kept the metal gate in a good state of repair, occasionally decorating it with paint supplied by the parish council, and keeping the lock and hinges well oiled and in good working condition.

The pound was Hubert's pride and joy and the parish council, along with the entire population of the village, was quite happy he had taken it into his loving care. It was the best kept pound in the locality, even if it was no longer used for its intended purpose. The idea of converting it into a peaceful little garden with seats had not yet been floated and I often wondered whether Hubert would agree to such a drastic change of status. There were times I thought he was just a little too possessive about 'his' pound; I don't think he liked the idea of other people using it, even though officially it was there for everyone's benefit.

Then, quite unexpectedly one April, the pound found itself back in use for its proper purpose. During the previous few weeks, there had been reports of a strange animal roaming the extremities of the village at night. Reports were inevitably sketchy because no one had caught a definitive sighting of the creature. All that had been noted was that it was black and that it managed to keep itself out of sight for most of the time.

Very occasionally someone had seen fleeting movements behind hedges and walls, and among trees in nearby woodlands. One report had recorded it moving among pine trees in a nearby plantation, most of such reports coming from passing motorists. They had caught the merest of glimpses in their headlights, always without actually seeing the entire creature. Brief flashes of it moving through the trees or behind hedgerows, usually with the light catching its eyes, were all that we had, but no one had ventured a suggestion as to what it might be. Some reports suggested a black panther, others that it was nothing more than a very large dog, or a black pig, or perhaps a wild deer; fallow deer can sometimes be coloured black. One man even thought it might be something that had escaped from a circus, like a black bear, or from a zoo – a gorilla perhaps? Whatever it was, it managed to keep itself mainly out of sight and it appeared quite capable of living in the wild, allowing only short flashes of its moving bulk to be spotted in the darkness. There was talk of hunting it down, but it appeared to move swiftly through the landscape, being sighted at widely differing locations which suggested it did not have a lair or permanent home. Seeking its footprints wasn't easy either because the land around the village, and indeed most of the woodland paths, were riddled with the ill-defined and partially obscured prints from cows, deer, sheep, dogs, horses and even humans. Identifying an alien print in such conditions was virtually impossible – what was needed was a firm sighting of the entire creature, with a photograph if possible. Few of the village stalwarts felt inclined to go looking for it – they had no wish tackle it or approach it on the grounds it could be dangerous. If it was something like a panther or black bear, it would probably not take kindly to human beings chasing it or frightening it. Such creatures could kill an unwary person. Because it might retaliate violently, some experts thought it best to leave it alone in the belief that if it was a foreign animal of some kind, it would not survive for long in the alien environment of the North York Moors. The general feeling was that nature would take care of it in due course.

As the stories began to spread, however, they grew more alarming at each telling with people starting to speculate wildly about its identity. What emerged was that people living both on the outskirts and in the village itself were not reporting any attacks on their livestock, other than by foxes. The work of foxes among lambs and poultry was easily recognized by country people, so this creature did not appear to be killing for food. Whatever it was, it did not seem to be carnivorous which would rule out a panther or even a large dog. Inevitably it became known as the Beast of Aidensfield, but with such sketchy impressions gained by little more than fleeting glimpses of the beast, it was by no means certain that it actually existed. Could the sightings be relied upon? Or were people's imaginations stronger than their common sense? Were they seeing only shadows or reflections of some kind? Or were some of the reports mischievous, simply told to gullible audiences to keep the story running?

It became the main topic of conversation in the village. The pub, post office and shop were all rich with fresh tales of momentary sightings of the black creature and eventually I was informed.

Just as we made notes of people who claimed to have seen flying saucers and other UFOs, I kept notes of sightings of the Beast of Aidensfield. Not everyone reported them directly to me, so there was no positive or accurate list of sightings, but whatever the creature was, it was never spotted in the village main street or indeed among the houses. Every sighting was beyond the houses, in the woods and plantations where trees were plentiful and where the season's new foliage might offer some protective cover. To my knowledge, it had not been seen on the open moor either, which suggested it was spending its time very close to human habitation, but not actually in the village. Perhaps it was finding shelter in disused farm buildings? When livestock was not using the fields around the village, the interconnecting gates were often left open to make it easier for farm vehicles to pass from one field to another without the need to stop on every journey to open, then shut, every gate. And gates leading into green lanes were likewise often left open when livestock was not using the pastures, so was this beast taking advantage of that? Was it wandering through the fields, taking shelter in the woods or disused buildings scattered across the landscape, or was it capable of leaping fences, gates and walls to pass from one pasture to another? As a panther might do. We had no idea; we could only make guesses.

The local newspaper got wind of the story and the *Ashfordly Gazette* published an article with headlines announcing THE BEAST OF

AIDENSFIELD, along with highly dramatized accounts from some witnesses. There was also a map of the area where sightings had been recorded.

All the witnesses described a large black beast which crept about the countryside at night in a stealthy manner, stalking the fields around the village and sometimes allowing itself to be glimpsed in the headlights of passing vehicles. Sadly, no one could supply a photograph, and no one had a sufficiently good view of the beast to be able to provide a clear description. The news item served only to increase speculation about the nature of the animal, and to frighten many Aidensfield residents into remaining indoors during the hours of darkness.

Then, one fine Sunday morning with the sun shining brightly, a small cow was seen walking down the village street. It was heading towards the church, stopping every so often to nibble at the grass of the village green. It was a miniature cow which looked to be about half the size of a breed like the Friesian and yet it appeared to be mature because it carried a useful pair of horns. And it was completely black.

With the church turning out, and many of its congregation being farmers or stock-keepers, it didn't take long for a group of men to decide it should be placed somewhere safe until its owner could be traced. And what better place than the village pound? Someone rang to alert me to this rural drama and when I walked along the street, I found the farmers were gently ushering the calm little cow towards the pound where Hubert had somewhat grudgingly unlocked the gate. It was now standing wide open to admit its first guest in years. I was amazed at the tiny size of the cow, but it seemed to be in good condition and not at all distressed.

'I can't say I relish the idea of having cattle in this pound,' he said to me. 'I've spent a lot of time mowing that grass inside, it's as neat as a lawn now and when that cow gets walking around, it'll make a mess and churn it up until it's a quagmire.'

'I don't think you've any choice,' I told him. 'Officially, the pound is still functioning and the Highways Act of 1959 still says that straying animals have to be impounded in what the law called the common pound. Its purpose is still to accommodate stray cattle until the owner is found. And that's the job of the pinder. That's you, I believe.'

'Me? I'm not the official pinder, there isn't

one now.'

'But you describe yourself as the pinder, Hubert, and I've seen your name in the parish magazine as the person responsible for the pound. Everyone knows you have made yourself responsible for it and as the person who placed the animal in the pound, you have to provide food, water and bedding for it and you must recover any expenses from the owner, when he or she is found. If you don't give it food and water, you could be prosecuted under the Protection of Animals Act of 1911, for cruelty.'

'But ... but ... I mean, well, it could be here for ages! And how am I supposed to find its owner? And what does it eat? And where do I find the food?'

'Well, you could ring the local paper to say the Beast of Aidensfield is now locked up in the village pound. That should get a story in the paper, or you could contact the local cattle mart to see who's bought a miniature cow in recent weeks; then there's that rare breeds establishment on the road to Eltering.'

'Rare breed? Does that mean it's valuable? I'm not sure about the insurance for valuable animals.'

'It looks like a rare breed to me; it's certainly not a common breed of cow, Hubert. I'd say that the sooner you find the owner, the less mess it will make in here and the sooner you'll be able to recover expenses and get rid of the animal. You can always get hay from a local farmer, to get things moving.'

'You're serious, aren't you, Mr Rhea?'

'Well, somebody has to do it, Hubert. You're a very reliable sort of person, a good citizen, but if you feel incapable of tracing the owner, then I shall have to set the ball rolling, but the responsibility for bedding and food rests with you. That's the law.'

'Incapable? Me? Of course I'm not incapable, not with my wealth of administrative experience. Leave it with me, Mr Rhea, and I shall produce a result! And I shall make sure that little animal is given food, water and bedding.'

That same Sunday lunchtime, I paid an official visit to the village pub where Claude Jeremiah Greengrass was holding court in his usual fashion. He was sitting on a bar stool with a glum expression on his face when Oscar Blaketon spotted my arrival.

'Ah, Nick, just the fellow. Claude here is rather upset. Tell him, Claude.'

'I've lost a valuable cow, Constable. A

little black one, female, a Dexter. Smallest breed in this country, like a dwarf. Quite rare. I think somebody must have nicked it and was just discussing it with Oscar, deciding whether I should report it.'

'Yours is it?' I asked.

'Well, not exactly, I'm looking after it for a few weeks, for a mate of mine who's in hospital. She's only a tiny cow, Constable...'

'You wouldn't have been letting it stray on the highway, by any chance, would you?' I put to him with a look of seriousness on my face.

'Well, not deliberately, no. But she's so tiny she gets through gaps in the hedges that no other cow would dream of doing. I've one heck of a job keeping her in; I'm running round my fences fixing holes I never knew existed...'

'You know you can be fined for allowing livestock to stray on the highway?' I persisted, not reminding him that the current fine was only five shillings per animal.

'Aye, well, it's not deliberate. If she's got out and on to the roads, it's not for the want of trying to keep her fenced in.'

'Well, Claude, if I were you, I'd pop along to the common pound because there's a very nice little black cow in there. She's just been impounded by Hubert Braithwaite and he's about to pay money for fodder, water and bedding, and he might levy a charge for use of the pound too. So if you don't want to be fined, and don't want to run up a bill with the pinder, you'd better get yourself along there right now, before my sergeant hears about your livestock straying on the highway.'

So Claude rushed along to the pound and recovered the little Dexter before Hubert could expend money on its care. Very light on its feet, the little animal had not made much of a mess inside, certainly its tiny hoofs had not churned up Hubert's precious patch of grass and so the pound remained unsullied.

Claude promised he would make sure she was enclosed in a secure Dexter-proof compound with not even the tiniest hole through which she might escape.

From that time, we never heard any more stories of the Beast of Aidensfield. Whether the sightings had been of that little cow wandering around at night will never be known with any certainty but I suspect that is what the witnesses had seen even if the tales had been embellished somewhat. A few years later, there were some wonderful tales of the Wild Cow of Aidensfield. Stories of Greengrass's little wandering cow looked set to be transformed into a local legend.

Story-telling has been with us since humans first began to communicate with one another, and a good tale will always survive the test of time. That's how folk stories survive; in spite of telling and re-telling, either verbally or in writing, they are passed down the generations, sometimes being adapted for the present time. No one ever seems willing to stop telling ancient, well-known tales and almost certainly they are added to, expanded and embellished with every new airing. I suppose the tales of Robin Hood are a good example of a never-ending yarn even if no one knows with any certainty whether or not he truly existed. Some long-running stories can conceal the truth too – think of Dick Turpin, the highwayman. The account of his stunning ride from London to York on Black Bess has become a legendary tale but the truth is he never undertook that journey. It was actually achieved by another highwayman called John Nevison, otherwise known as Swift Nick.

Turpin's bogus achievement arose when

an author called William Harrison Ainsworth accredited the feat to Turpin in his 1830s' book *Rookwood*, which was a work of fiction. Because the tale has entered the public consciousness, few people know the truth, and so the fable continues to be told as if it is genuine. No amount of correction will rectify the matter. There was nothing romantic about Turpin either – he was a thoroughly evil man, a rogue, murderer and a nasty and disgraceful piece of work.

I refer to these stories simply to show that a good rumour fuelled by skilled story-telling can often smother the truth. I was reminded of this when I heard that John Robert Holgate, a single man aged twenty-four and a petty thief from Ashfordly, had suddenly and inexplicably decided to go straight and abandon his life of mediocre crime. He was well known to the police of Ashfordly and district due to his dodgy character and persistent thieving. A pale-faced young man with a mop of unruly reddish-brown hair, and a rather thin stooping figure, he was described in police records as a labourer. It was amazing how many labourers had a police record – I suspect that most who described themselves as labourers when in police custody did very little or no work at all. The reality was that that labouring was something John Robert could never do. He lacked the necessary drive, strength and stamina, one of his main handicaps being his difficulty getting out of bed. In truth, like so many who claimed to be labourers, he had no profession or trade whatever.

He lived in a council house with his long-suffering parents who fed him, washed his clothes and gave him pocket money from their own limited earnings. To acquire extra money he exploited the dole system, stole cash from charity boxes in pubs or churches and conducted regular spells of shoplifting or buying and selling second-hand goods. There were several occasions when he conned old folks into giving him cash by fake hard luck stories, and in general he was a despicable nuisance, a proverbial thorn in the flesh of the police and law-abiding society of Ashfordly. He'd been to court several times, usually escaping with a warning to behave followed by a small fine, or yet another period of probation. He had somehow escaped serious punishment.

When appearing before the magistrates, he would always plead he was looking for work, but that no one would employ him.

That was true – they wouldn't because the business people of Ashfordly knew John Robert well enough not to trust him to do a full and honest day's work. He and his weaknesses were far too well known around town.

It follows that his momentous decision to go straight was the talk of the town, especially in the pub where he spent a lot of his time playing darts and getting drunk. In fact, that's where I first heard the story. During an occasional spell of duty in Ashfordly, I had called at the pub early one evening when the landlord hailed me and said, 'Heard about young Holgate, Mr Rhea?'

'John Robert, you mean?'

'The same.'

'No, what's he done now? Raided a building society or gone into the big time by breaking into the Bank of England?'

'No, he's going straight. And there's more! He's suddenly got it into his head to go climbing in the Himalayas and he's gone off to join an expedition. It'll take nine months, he reckons, including a bit of training.'

'You're joking!'

'No, I'm not. It's all over town. I know it's amazing but it's true, he came in to tell us all about it.'

He then told me the full tale. I knew some villains could suddenly see the error of their criminal ways and become priests or social workers, but the idea of John Robert being a serious mountaineer seemed highly unlikely. It was even more unlikely than him abandoning his life of low-key crime. But it seemed the tale was true. The landlord's story was supported by the regulars who were in the pub when I called, and in my presence they drank a toast to the success of John Robert. It seems he'd been thinking about it for some time, and after reading something in a newspaper about a forthcoming expedition, he'd rung the organizer and much to his own surprise, had been accepted.

And so tales of the forthcoming exploits of John Robert Holgate began to circulate the town. I am sure the accounts became exaggerated as they were repeated in Holgate's favourite pubs and haunts. The *Gazette* even published a front-page article saying that an Ashfordly man, John Robert Holgate, was going to tackle an unconquered peak in the Himalayas, adding it would publish a full personal account of his adventure upon his return.

We all waited with bated breath. I wondered what we would learn about all this at the end of those nine months. I remember thinking it was highly unlikely that such a useless specimen of humanity would suddenly change his character in such a dramatic manner. Apparently he had told his mother, father and sisters, and many of his pals in the pubs, that an Anglo-French expedition was being planned to climb the peak. To add strength to his story, he had shown them cuttings from some national newspapers. John Robert further enhanced his story by saying he had been in touch with the organizers who were looking for volunteer helpers and porters and, after visiting their headquarters in London, he'd been interviewed and accepted. His parents knew he'd been away quite a lot in recent times, catching the train or bus to distant places, or even hitch-hiking, and he told them those journeys had all been part of the selection procedure.

I then learned how John Robert caught a train south, and his family, by that time extremely proud, had stood on the platform at Ashfordly to watch him depart. I have no doubt there were tears in their eyes. He had assured them he would return in triumph, explaining that his first job was to be issued with his equipment then undertake some basic training. That would prepare him for his trek across the world so that he would become an important member of that Anglo-French expedition.

As the train was pulling into the platform, John said, 'I'll do my best to keep in touch but the mail isn't all that reliable from those mountain slopes. All that snow, you understand, and thousands of square miles of wilderness. But if I achieve this, it will prove I am capable of doing worthwhile things.'

He stood at the window of the carriage with his luggage at his feet, and there were further floods of tears as the Holgate family waved him off into the great unknown. Mum and Dad were already having fantasies of their son standing in the snow on the top of a famous mountain clutching the Union Jack. His picture would be in all the newspapers. John Robert would be world famous! They were so very proud of their son.

In the days which followed, most national newspapers carried photographs of the expedition departing from London with its vehicles and equipment, the first stage being to head for Paris to join their French counterparts. There was no picture of John Robert, however, the only photographs being of the leaders and their sponsors, not the more lowly team members like porters and supporters. Public interest was such that Mr and Mrs Holgate bought a scrapbook in which to paste newspaper cuttings of the expedition's progress, no doubt believing their son would feature in some of the forthcoming reports.

John Robert's remarkable decision deeply impressed the people of Ashfordly, so much so that one of the pubs he used decided to maintain a cuttings book plus a wall map of the expedition's proposed route. Little blue flags would be pinned to it to show its daily progress as announced in the newspapers, on television or on radio. In that way, the regulars and indeed visitors could follow John Robert's progress. Even at that early stage, it was planned that when John Robert returned with tales of his adventure, he would be hailed as a conquering hero and there would be a wonderful 'Welcome Home' party.

But tragedy was to follow. As the expedition was negotiating the foothills, the weather suddenly worsened. Fierce snowstorms and gales followed by a sudden warm spell caused the fallen snow to soften and become loose resulting in an avalanche which had roared down one of the mountain slopes. It overwhelmed the expedition and several members were swept to their deaths. Due to the difficulties of communication from such a remote region, it was impossible to gain an accurate and up-to-date account of the drama but the world's news networks were doing their utmost. It was a major news sensation around the world and it seemed inevitable that the expedition would be called off.

For the people of Ashfordly, and for the Holgate family in particular, this was the worst news they could have expected. Quite suddenly, the unknown plight of John Robert was on everyone's lips and in everyone's mind; his fate was under discussion in the pubs and clubs and even those who thought he was little more than a man-sized rat now found themselves having some grudging respect for him. To give him credit, the lad had sincerely tried to better himself. But now, no one knew whether he was dead or alive.

With no news filtering through, all his family and the townspeople could do was wait. In news items which followed the tragedy, there were no names of the victims and no details of the nationalities of those who had died. It was stressed that it could be some time before that kind of information was forthcoming. That was due to the remoteness of the area and the difficulties of communication. Difficulties were also expected in getting the victims formally identified but everything possible was being done to expedite those matters.

Eventually one of the English national newspapers – *The Times* – published a list of the British people who were known to have joined the expedition before it had left for Paris – but the name of John Robert Holgate was not among them. By chance, I was undertaking a two-hour spell of office duty in Ashfordly Police Station that same morning. The door opened and in walked Reg Holgate, John Robert's father. He looked extremely upset and anxious – at that point I had not read the list of names although I knew of the tragedy. Reg explained his worries, saying nothing had been heard of John Robert since leaving Ashfordly, his name was not among those known to have left the UK for the Himalayas, and Reg was therefore very concerned about his son. He had brought a copy of *The Times* with him so I read the article and gained the impression that not everyone was mentioned – the piece did stress that others had joined the expedition at different stages. That list was merely those who had joined in London at the very beginning; it was known that some had joined at Dover and others at Paris, so the list was far from complete.

'I'll see what I can do,' I promised Reg. 'I'll contact Interpol to see what kind of help is being organized, and how the international communications network is coping. Positive information should be available somewhere by now, but in cases like this, there are always delays and frustrations. I know that doesn't sound very helpful, but I'm afraid you'll just have to be patient. You can be sure things will be happening out there, and everyone will be notified in due course.'

'Aye,' said Reg. 'Aye, I know, Mr Rhea, but I thought I'd better get things moving, with not hearing anything about our John Robert.'

'Wait a few minutes, Reg; I'll ring Interpol while you're here then you'll be as up-to-date as possible. If they can't assist, you might get help from the newspapers or someone like Red Cross, or even the expedition's own organizers, whoever they are. *The Times* will also have a contact number, I'm sure.'

Interpol was not a glamorous world-wide

police force as many people thought. It was an office. Its full name is International Criminal Police Commission and its headquarters was originally in Vienna, but after the Second World War, it moved to Paris. In England, it had an office in New Scotland Yard's building, a part of the department known as C.5(2). Interpol was really a clearing house for crime, keeping records of international criminals, their fingerprints, methods of operation and so forth. Its officers, however, were always willing to give help and advice on other matters of an international police nature. I spoke to an inspector and explained my enquiry, but he said his organization was not able to help with such a specialized non-police incident, but he told me that New Scotland Yard itself was co-ordinating enquiries in England and Wales so far as deaths of our nationals were concerned. The section of Department C.1 which dealt with international matters such as passports, immigration and extradition and which maintained contacts with embassies across the world, was the office to ring. He provided the number and I rang it to find myself speaking to a detective inspector.

I explained my enquiry and he listened, then said, 'Yes, PC Rhea, we have a list of

English and Welsh members of the Anglo–French expedition; Scotland is looking after its own. We're in constant touch with the French authorities, and those from Nepal and Tibet. The Nepalese and Tibetans are accustomed to this kind of thing happening in their countries and always do their best to provide up-to-date information about casualties. They know exactly what's needed. I have the complete list of UK members who joined the expedition – it's on my desk right now – and your John Robert Holgate is not among them.'

'Really? He told his family he was joining the expedition.'

'That doesn't surprise me. I suspect he's one of several who told that kind of yarn to impress girlfriends or families. It's quite common.'

'Is it?' I must have sounded rather naïve to the man in Scotland Yard.

'As sure as eggs is eggs, PC Rhea. We have a list of all UK personnel who joined the expedition, abstracted from the expedition's own files and confirmed by their passports. So, what else do you know about John Robert Holgate?'

'He's a local lad,' I said, remembering that his father was standing only a few feet away from me, listening to my end of this conversation. 'From Ashfordly in the North Riding of Yorkshire,' and I gave his age and home address. 'He's had a huge change of direction; he is known to us here at the police station, but his family tell me he's had a big change of attitude.'

'Am I right in thinking his family are with you?' Clearly he had recognized my cautious and careful choice of words.

'Right,' I said. 'His father is with me now, trying to find out what's happened to him.'

'And he can't hear my voice?'

'Right,' I confirmed.

'Good. Just let me do a few more checks in our records,' he said, adding, 'criminal records, I mean. If he's known to you in the way I think you mean, he'll be in our National Criminal Record Office files. It'll take a few minutes. Give me your number and I'll call you back.'

'He's going to check and ring me back in a few minutes,' I told Reg, when I replaced the handset. 'Do you fancy a coffee while you're waiting?'

I brewed some coffee, chiefly because I wanted one, and settled Reg in a chair in the enquiry office. He didn't say much, his face showing his deep concern for the plight of his son. I knew he must have found it difficult to come and ask for help like this, the family not having much respect or time for the police, probably due to the frequent arrests of John Robert, so I tried to make him feel as comfortable as I could. I sat in another chair and we chatted about unimportant matters such as the exploits of Middlesbrough football team. After about twenty minutes, the telephone rang. It was my contact from Scotland Yard.

'Well, PC Rhea,' he said quietly. 'I have some good news and some bad news. Which do you want first?'

'I'll have the good news,' I said, watching the reaction on Reg's face.

'John Robert Holgate is alive and well.'

'Thank God for that. So where is he?'

'Northallerton Prison,' he said. 'Doing nine months for theft. It seems he was caught shoplifting in York some time ago, arrested in possession of the stolen goods and seen nicking them by both the store detective and a local bobby. There was no way he could talk his way out of that one and his previous record guaranteed him a short custodial sentence. I think he knew what he was facing which is why he went off with his suitcase packed. He was sentenced at York, by the way. Seems he never got to London, or Dover, or the Himalayas.'

'He said he would be gone for nine months,' I said.

'It seems to me, PC Rhea, that when he left home, your John Robert knew he was going down for nine months and went prepared to disappear from the face of the earth for that period of time. He's obviously had good advice from somebody, that's for sure, and he's told a wonderful yarn to explain his absence. A neat trick – it might have worked if that avalanche hadn't happened. He could have returned home as a hero!'

'Thanks,' I said, now having the awful task of providing Reg with the truth. He listened with increasing disbelief as I explained about his wayward son, and then he stormed out, saying, 'When he gets back here, I'll wring his neck ... so help me...'

'Why not go and visit him?' I shouted, as he raced down the police-station path to tell his family. 'And tell him you know what he's done.'

'You bet I will ... he'll never want to come back here by the time I've finished with him.'

I wondered if John Robert would ever dare to return to Ashfordly now that his deception had become known. His pals in the pubs, not to mention his family, would make sure he regretted every moment of his cunning plan. In fact, he did not return. I think his father firmly impressed upon him that he was no longer welcome at the family home, stressing that when he was released he would have to make his own way in the world by finding work and accommodation as far away from Ashfordly as possible. John Robert left Ashfordly on his release, but I don't know where he settled.

In spite of their anger and disillusionment, Reg and his family never told anyone that John Robert had set off to go to prison, and not to climb the Himalayas as everyone had believed. They never spoke about him afterwards.

Even today, some people in Ashfordly speak of the brave John Robert Holgate who set off for the Himalayas and perished in an avalanche, never to return either dead or alive. Such is the power of a good story. I can envisage that at some time in the future, John Robert might even be remembered by a plaque on his home or perhaps a statue in the park.

Chapter 10

If the incident with John Robert Holgate and his supposed expedition to the Himalayas left any lingering impressions upon me, it was the fact his family were so very proud of him when they thought he was trying to achieve something worthwhile. I am sure their anger really disguised deeper feelings of dismay and utter disappointment when he let them down, but I remember thinking that family bonds might eventually lead them to attempt a reconciliation.

The strength of the family unit was very impressive among those living on and around the moors which formed my beat. Because many were farmers, they relied on lots of willing hands at peak periods such as haymaking, potato-picking and the corn harvest, and this help came freely from family members – sons, daughters, cousins, half-cousins, nephews, nieces, in-laws and anyone else with a link of some kind. At harvest-time, farmers helped each other when necessary, a system which had prevailed for centuries. It was that kind of help which spawned the Mell Supper after the last sheaf had been cut – really nothing more than a big thank-you party for the helpers. Naturally, after that kind of hard work, there were lots of parties.

Even into the early years of the twentieth century, many farmers had huge families, it being considered sensible because the lads would grow up to work around the farm instead of Dad having to employ hired hands. The girls would blossom into capable young women who would learn how to milk the cows, make butter and cheese, mend clothes and cook gigantic meals. There was no point in paying money for other people to do things which could be done by the family.

Just prior to the 1960s, the thought of farmers' male offspring doing anything other than joining the family business was regarded as muddled thinking, and it was just as silly to expect farm lasses not to marry into another farming family. That's how farms were perpetuated and passed from father to son or family to family *ad infinitum*. But within a short time after the Second World War, farm lads were realizing there was an easier living to be made by doing other work with shorter hours, less hassle, and more money, while offering remarkable things called holidays and days off. Farm girls thought likewise and so youngsters began to seek work elsewhere.

The advent of specialized machinery which would cope with most jobs about the farm helped to lessen the impact of this increasing shortage of labour and so, in a way, I worked in the countryside while it was undergoing transition. I saw bright farmers' lads put modern ideas to their fathers, only to be told they would never work – and so the lads left farming. Similarly, I saw intelligent young woman tell their mums and dads they had no wish to spend their entire lives feeding hens, cooking meals and coping with harvest and haymaking, all without a holiday or a day off. And yet, some farmers stuck resolutely and even defiantly to their former ways, believing that the family was vital for the survival of traditional farming in England.

One of them was Miles Harland from Stoneyridge Farm at Thackerston. He and his hard-working wife, Sally, owned a large hilltop spread above the village which had spectacular views across the dale below. It was very windswept, but the farmhouse was in the midst of the outbuildings which provided useful shelter from the worst of the moorland weather.

Miles, approaching fifty, specialized in hardy livestock such as black-faced moorland sheep and South Devon cattle. He kept the South Devons for their beef and used Ayrshire cows for their milk yield. He was known as a skilled breeder, showing regularly around Yorkshire and further afield where he won lots of awards. Not only was he a skilled breeder of livestock, however, he was also a skilled breeder of children because he had fifteen, ranging from 2-year-old Emily to 24-year-old George with many others in between. Miles believed in passing his farm down to his sons and he also believed that his family should help around the place at all times in all weathers. I don't think he had bargained on having so many children, so if he wanted them all to prosper on the farm, it meant years of hard work building up the business. There would obviously have to be diversification of some kind if it was to support such a lot of people. In the meantime, his sons had to learn their craft, just as he'd had to. Fortunately, the farm was thriving due to his efforts, but to maintain it in that condition meant no one could slacken in their endeavours.

I was never sure how many lads there were in his family, or how many daughters because I seldom saw them all in one place at the same time. In spite of their numbers, the homestead was always brimming with happiness and activity. Everyone seemed to get along with one another and their parents, probably because the hard-worked Sally was always cheerful and pleasant. In her mid-forties, she was a lovely woman with a warm, round face, rich dark hair, a rather plump figure and an apparent permanent air of calm in spite of the frantic activity around her.

Then one day in August, I called to complete my usual quarterly examination of the stock register, and after I'd signed it in Miles's office in one of the outbuildings, Sally called me into the kitchen. As I walked across the foldyard, I could see lots of young people about the place, probably all of whom were her children.

'I'll get you some tea and piece of cake,' she said, before I could decline, and within moments, I was sitting at the kitchen table with a massive mug in front of me and an equally massive chunk of fruit loaf. Children were all around, some passing through the kitchen, some playing outside with older ones, some working or otherwise occupying themselves in the spacious buildings. As ever, the place was a hive of activity.

'I've a problem, Nick. Now if you look out of the window, you'll see a little lad playing out there. The one with fair hair and a red shirt; he's about four years old.'

I looked out and spotted the child in question. He was galloping about with a crowd of others, playing some kind of noisy game. 'I can see him,' I said.

'Do you know who he is?' she asked.

'No,' I responded, wondering if he had a famous mother or father, or if he'd recently featured in one of the local newspapers for any reason.

'Neither do I,' she shrugged. 'And neither do the children. That's the problem; I've no idea who he is or where he's come from. I thought I'd better mention it to you.'

'So where has he come from?' I asked the logical question.

'I've no idea, and I don't know how long he's been here either.'

'You don't know how long he's been here?' I couldn't really believe that. How could a mother not know there was a stranger among her brood?

'Not the faintest,' she grinned. 'You see, our older ones look after the younger ones, they've all got their jobs. Three days ago, it was Ralph's birthday party, he was five. He had lots of friends here, as you can imagine, and the other young ones had their own friends too. It was like Bedlam. When it was all over, the mums or dads came to collect their offspring. That little lad's been left behind, but I've no idea where he's come from or who he is.'

'So he's been living here without anyone noticing?'

'Well, yes. The children saw him at breakfast over the last few days and at bedtime and so on, but they all thought I'd asked him to stay. I saw him too, but thought one of my lot had invited him. They do that sort of thing very regularly. We all help each other – we have to, getting him up, putting him to bed, bathtime, finding fresh clothes, all that sort of thing. We've plenty of such things in the house – enough to equip an army. When I saw him this morning, I realized I'd not rung round to see if he belongs to anyone. No one has been ringing about him though. To be honest, I don't know who to ring. I've no idea who his parents are. The children invite their own friends and they just turn up. I've no time to go doing their inviting for them, but when I asked after breakfast, none of mine said they'd invited him. They don't know who he is either.'

'It's odd no one's been asking about him. Even if you didn't notice him at first, you'd think his mother would have missed him and done something about it. She must have known he was coming to the party.'

'Unless she has a big family like mine. You never miss one or two, not unless you get them all to stand still for a few moments while you count heads.'

'So what's his name?' I had to sound efficient and practical now.

'He says it's Hugh, at least that's what it sounds like, he doesn't speak very well and doesn't know his surname, or his address. He seems quite happy to stay here and it is school holidays, but, joking aside, there must be a mum somewhere who's missing a child. I wondered if you'd had any reports?'

'Not in the last few months and certainly not in the last few days. If one had been reported missing, we'd have known, it would have been circulated over a very wide area.'

'So what can I do?'

'We need to find out who brought him,'

was my first bright idea. 'Which of yours was it who was having the birthday party?'

'Ralph, it was his fifth. He's not at school yet, he starts in September, but he goes to a playgroup in Thackerston, so he has quite a circle of little friends. Those of mine nearest to him in age are allowed to bring their friends too, so some who go to the local school turned up and so did others who go to different schools. Most of them live in Thackerston, or fairly close by.'

'So really, Sally, you've no idea how many came to Ralph's party?'

'Not really, no. It was just a big crowd of children, just as it always is. My job is to get them settled down at table and feed them; they manage to get the older ones to help with things like games and competitions.'

'I suppose it's rather like the boss of a big firm not knowing who the tea-lady is, or who appointed that big blonde in the photocopying room?'

'Yes, I suppose so, something like that, although I've never worked in an office or factory. Just on farms, my dad's and now this one.'

'Can you give me some idea of the families whose children were invited to Ralph's party?'

'I can get out my list of local addresses, we use it for Christmas cards and so on, that might help.'

Her household administration seemed to be well organized because she went over to an old desk in a corner of the vast kitchen, pulled out a foolscap book and opened it. It was a list of all her personal contacts, family, friends and local businesses, and it contained their addresses and telephone numbers.

'If you can give me a list of possible names,' I suggested. 'I'll go and visit them. If this child is genuinely lost, then it's my responsibility to do something about it. And I reckon you won't really have the time for all the extra work and worry that could be involved in finding out where he's come from.'

'That would be a big help,' she smiled. 'Yes, thank you.'

'And can this little lad remain until I get this sorted out? I'd hate to put him into a home of any kind; he'll be far happier here; he looks very settled in.'

'Yes, I'd rather he stayed, I feel responsible. Besides, it would be awful if he had to be taken into a childrens' home.'

I went outside to speak to the child in the

hope I could elicit some useful information from him but didn't succeed. All he could tell me was that his name sounded like Hugh, but he had no idea of his surname or home address. I left Stoneyridge Farm with a list of party-going families who lived in the village and surrounding landscape. Glancing down the list, I realized I knew quite a lot of the people, several of whom were farming families I visited on a fairly regular basis.

Three on the list had more than eight children each and I thought they were the most likely starting points. Perhaps the children had arranged something among themselves. Perhaps Mum had thought little Hugh, or whatever his name was, had been invited to remain as a guest for two or three days? Clearly, there had been some kind of breakdown in communication.

My first call was the Porter family at Low Marsh Farm, also in Thackerston but when I spoke to Mrs Porter she shook her head.

'Sorry, Mr Rhea, five of mine went to the party, and we got them all back home safe and sound. None missing and no extra ones. Have you tried the Russells at Ashtree House? They often have cousins to stay during the school holidays.'

As the Russell household also had eight children and was on my list, I made it my next visit and, like so many of these farms, Mrs Russell was hard at work in the kitchen. She was baking bread.

She halted her pummelling of the dough as I rapped on the window, and with a flour-covered hand, beckoned me to enter. I explained the problem whereupon she pursed her lips, shook her head and said, 'Sorry, mine and a couple of cousins all came back, Mr Rhea. I've no idea who that little lad is.'

It was quite a long drive to the last of the three larger family homes, this being Cockpit Farm at Ploatby. As the name implied, this had been the venue of the cock-fighting fraternity many years earlier, at that time being an inn, and evidence of the former cockpit could still be seen in the field behind the house. Even now, the occasional old coin is found during ploughing, and not long ago, a set of gaffles was unearthed. Gaffles were steel spurs attached to the ankles of fighting birds so that they could inflict greater harm upon their opponents.

This spacious former inn was home to the Palliser family, Tom, Belinda and their brood of eight. Tom was a farmer but he also ran a fleet of cattle trucks which helped him meet the costs of rearing his large family. When I arrived he was working some distance down the fields. I found Belinda, as expected, in the kitchen preparing dinner, the local name for the midday meal. She invited me to stay, this being a custom on the moors; whenever a visitor called at a farm when there was a meal on the table, he or she was always invited – or even expected – to join in. But I said I must decline because I had to press on with this enquiry.

I explained the situation and she listened intently, then asked, 'Did you say he's called Hugh? A fair-haired lad?'

'Sally Harland isn't sure and his pronunciation isn't very clear,' I told her. 'He tried to tell me his name and it sounded rather like Hugh, but he doesn't know his surname or where he comes from.'

'I wonder if it's little Ewan?' she gasped. 'Oh, God, if it is, something must have happened to his mum...'

'Ewan?' I puzzled with some sense of relief. 'You know him?'

'We've had a little lad called Ewan staying with us, the son of an old schoolfriend of mine. Her husband was a sailor in the merchant navy but she's on her own now and works for a local solicitor. She couldn't get time off last week so I said Ewan could come here for a few days, until she had her own holiday from work. Because Ewan was here, I asked if he could go to Ralph Harland's party with our children. I spoke to one of the Harland children who said it would be fine. The Harlands are like that, everyone's welcome and they wouldn't notice an extra one. My friend's called Ann Page, by the way, and she lives at Scarborough.'

'So you took Ewan to the party?'

'Yes, my husband drove four of ours and little Ewan to Stoneyridge Farm, the arrangement being that Ann would collect Ewan direct from there. We would take him and she would collect him. That's what we decided, quite simple. She said she wouldn't have time to pop in and see me, so she would go straight to the Harland's farm and pick up Ewan after the party. If she hasn't done that, something must have gone wrong. She hasn't been in touch with me since then so I had no idea she might not have collected him.'

'Is she on the phone?' I asked. 'I could ring and check.'

'No, she's not. That's a problem just now.

She's in rented accommodation, temporarily she hopes as it's a small flat with a crusty old landlady. But now you mention it, Mr Rhea, she hasn't dropped me a postcard to say thanks for having Ewan. She's good at doing that, keeping in touch and expressing her thanks. So maybe something has gone dreadfully wrong?'

'So what about her husband? You said he's not with her now?'

'No, they got divorced nearly two years ago. He was always away at sea, and life wasn't easy. So they divorced. And both her parents are dead. I'm really worried now. It's very strange she's not been in touch, Mr Rhea, very strange indeed.'

I explained that in such cases, a policeman from the station closest to her home would be asked to go round and check that she was all right, and if so, pass on any message so that she could deal with the problem. Belinda said I could use her telephone because it would save time. I took a note of Ann's address and then rang Scarborough Police. The office duty constable answered.

'It's PC Rhea from Aidensfield,' I introduced myself, and then explained the story.

He listened carefully as I outlined the story, giving Ann Page's name and address and then he said, 'Hang on a minute, PC Rhea, we've an enquiry outstanding about a Mrs Ann Page from that address ... just a moment ... it's on a clip near the enquiry hatch...'

There was a rustling of paper and then he returned to the phone. 'She's in Scarborough Hospital, PC Rhea, with serious injuries. A bad traffic accident in her car, a lorry hit her on a crossroads. She's been unconscious ever since. We've been trying to find relatives but no-one knows her. Her landlady couldn't help. She's not been there long, although the old lady did say there was a child but that the child was away with friends, on holiday. We've not been able to interview Mrs Page, and no one's come forward to say they know her in spite of pleas in the local papers.'

'So what's her overall condition?'

'When we checked this morning, we were told she had stabilized, and it's expected she'll recover consciousness very soon, but she'll remain in hospital for at least three weeks, maybe longer. She's off the danger list, though.'

'It would seem we have her little son staying on a farm in this part of the world, although he doesn't know his own name or where he comes from. I'm speaking from a friend's house. Look, now I know her situation, I'll make some enquiries and see if I can get a positive identification of the little lad. I'll call you back when I've got something a bit more certain.'

So Belinda Palliser discovered that her friend was in a serious condition in hospital, and that little Ewan was enjoying himself at Stoneyridge Farm among a crowd of welcoming children. Belinda said she would take over the matter, first checking that the little boy at Stoneyridge Farm really was Ewan Page, and then she would arrange to go to Scarborough to visit Ann and speak to the hospital authorities about her.

She even promised to take Ann into her own home until she was fit to resume normal life. I relayed all this to Scarborough Police who were most relieved that we had found someone to care for Ann and Ewan. When I explained this to Sally Harland in another phone call from the Pallisers, she said little Ewan could stay as long as necessary; one more mouth to feed among her brood was not a problem. There was plenty of room for him, plenty of fresh clothes and a bed all of his own.

It was a typically nice reaction from a

family living on the North York Moors.

Another instance relating to a strong family background involved a lady known to everyone as Old Mrs Cummins. Her Christian names were Alice May and she was the widow of Matt Cummins who had been the farrier and blacksmith for Elsinby until his death some years prior to my arrival. Old Mrs Cummins lived alone in Greystone House, a large, handsome building not far from the Hopbind Inn. In former times, this had adjoined the blacksmith's workshop, now a private garage. The blacksmith's business and premises had been in Mrs Cummins's family for generations and she had married the man who'd been her father's apprentice. In time, he had moved into the family house, becoming its owner on the death of his father-in-law. Mrs Cummins's mother had moved into a smaller cottage at the distant end of the village, having the sense not to make a threesome of her daughter's marriage. There were two sons of the marriage between Matt and Alice, but neither had wanted to retain the blacksmith's business, both leaving home to find work elsewhere. Both were now living in the south of England.

When Matt died, therefore, Old Mrs Cummins lived alone in the big house and although her sons visited her from time to time, most of her life was spent without anyone else in the house, albeit with friends from the village popping in quite frequently. She was a nice old lady, very kind and affable, and could often be seen pottering down to the shop or post office and helping with Anglican church matters such as arranging the flowers or planning the cleaning rota. I was never quite sure how old she was, but my guess was that she was well into her eighties and it was fascinating to think she had lived in Greystone House for her entire life.

During my time as the village bobby at Aidensfield, with Elsinby being part of my beat, I would often encounter Old Mrs Cummins in the street and she was always keen to stop for a chat. She loved telling me about the old days, when the house was always attended by patient horses waiting to be shod, or farmers wanting her father to design and make a particular piece of equipment or tool. He was the sort of man who could fix anything or build anything, even things in brick, stone or wood. A very useful man to have in the centre of the village.

She was a small woman, only some five feet tall and very thin with a slight suggestion of a stoop. She had an unnerving habit of walking along the village street wearing little more than a thin short-sleeved blouse and light skirt, even in the coldest weather. I think she had an overcoat and cardigans in the house, but the chill of northern winters did not appear to affect her. There were times I worried about her being out of doors in that state because when a person is suffering from hypothermia they don't feel the cold. In fact, even with ice and snow around them, they tend to feel too warm, sometimes to the extent of throwing off their flimsy clothing as their body cools down.

I mentioned my concerns to the district nurse who was a regular caller at Greystone House, but in spite of our joint concern, Old Mrs Cummins ignored our advice. Over the months, I felt sure she was deteriorating. Instead of the quick movements I associated with her regular walks along the village, she appeared to be slower and more stooped. In short, age was taking its toll but she continued to walk in the flimsiest of clothing during the worst of the weather.

Then, one February morning, I was

undertaking an early morning patrol which meant I was in Elsinby at seven o'clock, remaining in the village for about an hour with the uniform on show. It was all part of our belief that showing ourselves in this way was a good public relations exercise as well as being valuable in preventing petty crime, whatever the time of day or night. It was a wet morning and very cold, typical of the month, but dawn had arrived even if the sun was not shining through the grey clouds. And then I noticed Old Mrs Cummins heading towards me as I stood outside the telephone kiosk. As usual, she was in her skirt and short-sleeved blouse, though the morning was bitterly cold and wet. I was reasonably warm and dry with my cape around my shoulders.

'Good morning, Constable.' She nodded her old grey head as she approached. 'Not a bad morning for the time of year.'

'Not at all, Mrs Cummins. So where are you off to at this time of day?'

'I'm going to see my mother, just to check she's all right,' she answered.

'Your mother?' I must have sounded both disbelieving and horrified because I knew her mother had been dead for a long, long time, probably thirty years or more.

'Yes, she lives at Brook Cottage now, you know. She likes me to pop in from time to time, just to see if she needs anything.'

'Well, I don't think she's in just now, so do you think it would be a good idea to go home and keep warm?'

'Are you sure, Mr Rhea? She's never usually out at this time of day.'

'Would you like me to check?' I asked. 'I could pop down there while you go home, and then you could put the kettle on and when I get back, we could have a nice cup of tea and a chat.'

'What a lovely idea, Mr Rhea, that is very kind of you. Yes, you do that. Tell Mother I will come later if she needs anything, and when you get back, we can have a lovely cup of tea and a chat, just you and me.'

'Would you like to borrow my cape? Just until you get home? It will keep you warm and dry.'

'Oh, no, Mr Rhea, I am quite warm, thank you, and a drop of rainwater never did anyone any harm. So, I will see you in a few minutes.'

As she turned on her heel, I wondered if my deception was warranted but I thought it was better than saying her mother was dead, at least for the time being. Somehow,

I must determine what was going on in her head.

As she headed home, I went along the street towards Brook Cottage, just in case she was watching to check my actions. It was a walk of about six or seven minutes and when I arrived, the man who now lived in the house, Jim Clarke, was leaving for work. I caught him in the drive and halted him.

'Morning, Jim. I won't detain you if you're off to work, but has Old Mrs Cummins been calling here recently?'

'Not to my knowledge, Mr Rhea. Why, is there a problem?'

'I've just found her wandering down the street, heading for your house. You know her mother lived here years ago?'

'Yes, she once told me.'

'Well, she was coming to visit her mother; she must still think her mum's living here.'

'Oh, dear. I'd better tell Jean, just in case she turns up. What should she do? Jean, I mean, if she turns up?'

'Just say her mother isn't here, and suggest she goes back home. I'll have words with Nurse Horsfield. If she's losing her marbles, she'll need looking after. Nurse Horsfield might have the sons' addresses.'

'I'll pop in and tell Jean now before I go to work,' said Jim, and off he went.

When I returned to Greystone House and knocked gently on the back door, Old Mrs Cummins responded but it was immediately evident she had forgotten all about our meeting only minutes earlier. 'Well, what a surprise, Mr Rhea, you calling at this time of the morning. Is something wrong?'

'Er, no,' I was momentarily lost for words because I was expecting our cup of tea and a chat. 'I was just passing and wondered if you were all right. I didn't see any smoke coming from your chimney and had heard you hadn't been too well recently.'

'Oh, you shouldn't take notice of other people, Mr Rhea, I just had a little cold, nothing to get worried about, but I'm fine. Absolutely fine. Now, would you like a cup of tea? I've just made one for breakfast and there's enough for two.'

She passed me a china cup of tea, but no biscuits, and we sat at the table where she had laid her breakfast. She said it was good of me to keep an eye on her but said she was perfectly all right while not once referring to her mother.

But I wanted to know whether the little incident in the street was just a blip of some kind, or whether I should alert Nurse Horsfield and Mrs Cummins's sons. We chatted for some time, and then I decided to raise the question of her mother's house.

'Didn't your mother live in the village after her retirement?' I asked when a suitable opportunity arose. 'At Brook Cottage?'

'Oh yes, Mr Rhea, she loved it there. It's much cosier than this rambling old place and there's a very nice young couple in there now. Maybe I should think about getting a smaller house, but at my time of life, I think I'd find it difficult to move: one does get settled in a place.'

I was quite satisfied she had forgotten all about her interrupted trip to Brook Cottage but after taking my leave, I decided I would alert the nurse. After all, if Old Mrs Cummins had taken to wandering off in search of her past, there was no telling where she might get to.

Later that morning I noticed Margot Horsfield's car parked outside a house and waited until she emerged.

'Hi, Margot, I'm glad I found you. I wanted a word.'

I told her about Old Mrs Cummins's momentary mental blip, and Margot said a single occasion was not of great concern, but if she had more of those lapses on a regular basis, coupled with more wanderings, then she would probably need care or treatment of some kind. Nonetheless, she assured me she would alert Mrs Cummins's sons about that little incident and warn them that their mother may be in need of family care in the near future.

Over the next few months, I saw Old Mrs Cummins quite regularly when I visited Elsinby and always made a point of chatting to her, chiefly to determine whether she was lucid or not. On most occasions, she was, but then one Thursday afternoon I saw her heading off down the village and hailed her as usual.

'Off for your daily walk, are you?' I asked.

'I'm going to see my mother,' she said. 'It's Thursday, Mr Rhea, and on Thursday afternoons she always goes to visit Miss Purnell for afternoon tea. Miss Purnell always said I was welcome to join them anytime I wanted, and so I thought I would pop along this afternoon.'

'And where does Miss Purnell live?' I asked.

'Well, you should know that, Mr Rhea, being the local policeman! She's lived there for years. Mulberry Cottage, not far from the church.'

I knew that Miss Purnell had died a long time ago, and that people called Sherwin now lived in her former house. There had been several occupants in the meantime. I was unsure how to make the dear old thing aware that both Miss Purnell and her mother were no longer alive. I didn't want to continue my earlier deception and felt it in the best interests of the old lady that she be told the truth.

'Er, Mrs Cummins,' I began, not quite knowing how to put it, 'I'm afraid Miss Purnell is dead...'

'Oh dear, I knew she hadn't been well. When's the funeral?'

'I don't know...'

'Well, in that case I mustn't go to the house and be a nuisance. I'm surprised Mother hasn't told me about this, but being a Thursday, she may be out somewhere else. She always goes down to the shop on Thursdays after visiting Miss Purnell but I have no intention of trekking all the way down there on the off-chance of catching her. You will let me know when the funeral is, won't you, Mr Rhea? I wouldn't want to miss it.'

And she turned on her heel and pottered

towards her own home. I rang Margot Horsfield later that evening to update her on the latest development in this growing saga, and she told me that Old Mrs Cummins had done similar things in recent weeks. In all cases, she had gone to houses which her mother was in the habit of visiting on regular occasions, some of those occasions being when Old Mrs Cummins was a small girl. In effect, she was reliving her childhood and youthful days, haunting places closely associated with her mother. Her father never seemed to feature in these outings, it was always her mother. The link between Old Mrs Cummins and her mother must have been particularly strong.

From a physical aspect, Old Mrs Cummins was quite capable of looking after herself in spite of those mental lapses. She could do her washing and ironing, cooking and baking, cleaning and letter writing, and her house was as neat and tidy as ever. But Nurse Horsfield felt that those relapses into her past were occurring with a greater frequency. It seemed that she experienced them when out and about in the village, but while at home her mind returned to the present day and so, if anyone called to see her, they saw nothing wrong with her. When her sons came to see her in response to Margot's calls, they found nothing wrong and, of course, Old Mrs Cummins would not go to live with either of them. Elsinby, and Greystone House in particular, was her home, and had been for the whole of her long life. All she was doing during those relapses, was revisiting her family haunts.

In short, there was nothing anyone could do. And throughout the whole of my service at Aidensfield, she continued to live at Greystone House and I would often see her heading off down the village street, *en route* to visit her mother at one place or another. It appeared, however, that when she arrived at those other houses, the fact that the door was answered by a stranger was enough to switch her back into modern-day mode. I often wondered if she thought she was living in a dream before waking up to find herself back at home.

She died sometime after I left Aidensfield and later I learned she had asked to be buried beside her mother. At the very end, therefore, mother and daughter were reunited.

I have no wish to give the impression that all families living in and around the moors were splendid examples of happiness and contentment. They were not; some were extremely dysfunctional, but I like to think those were in the minority. In thinking about families, of course, I had to be very aware of the needs of my own wife and four rapidly growing children and there were times I wondered if there were occasions that the demands of my police duty coupled with its irregular hours, night time and weekend work took precedence over family matters.

Certainly, one's constabulary duties must be done and it was the police culture of the time that the requirement to do one's duty must be foremost in our minds at all times. Even when off duty, on holiday, or having a day off to do some shopping, one could not ignore matters which demanded police attention. Off-duty police officers could not stand back and wait for other people to deal with emergencies such as traffic accidents, fires, drownings and vandalism; they were expected to do their duty by taking charge and dealing with the matter, even if it sometimes meant putting themselves at risk. I've known off-duty police officers deal with all manner of incidents, including tackling knife-wielding or axe-wielding maniacs; I've known them dash into burning buildings to rescue people or arrest shoplifters as they were legging it to supposed freedom with their loot. And more.

In the peace and solitude of Aidensfield, however, such dramas were very rare indeed, and I like to think the time I spent with my family was as much as any other father spent with his. Maybe my odd working hours meant I had more time with my children – when working night duty, for example, I had a lot of daytime hours at my disposal and even if I had to work at bank holidays such as Christmas or Easter, I was allowed time off in lieu which meant we could go out somewhere when there were fewer crowds.

Unofficially, the force, or those in charge at local level, always did their best to consider police families over the Christmas period. Obviously, the job had to continue twenty-four hours a day, every day, but it was the practice for village constables, such as myself, to spend Christmas Day at home, even when on duty. We would don our uniforms, ring in to the sub-divisional office to report on duty at 9 a.m., and then spend the day at home with the family. We were there if required because it had to be understood that if an incident arose, we were duty-bound to attend, even if it occurred in the middle of opening the presents around the tree or eating Christmas dinner. In fact, the chances of something dramatic happening on Christmas Day were slender because most people were at home, celebrating this great religious and family festival.

One Christmas Day I was enjoying that kind of relaxed atmosphere. It was a fine, sunny day but very cold with a northerly wind. Snow had been forecast for the moors during the Christmas period, but so far none had arrived. It meant the roads were clear and there was not likely to be an interruption of our power supply unless the winds grew stronger and blizzards developed. Officially, I was on duty, my brief to be responsible for all the rural beats in the Ashfordly section should anything happen. I had booked on at 9 a.m. and was wearing my uniform shirt and trousers, but was at home helping with the Christmas dinner and playing with the excited children as they unwrapped their presents. Father Christmas had been during the night but there were more presents beneath the tree, all awaiting an opening session before we ate. Despite the family atmosphere, I was ready for action if necessary and, of course, I could not drink alcohol in case I was called out. At five o'clock that evening, another constable would take over my responsibilities, and he would also remain at home unless called out. After five, therefore, I could raise a glass to toast our good health over Christmas.

When Mary announced that our Christmas dinner was ready, we all gathered around the table, pulled the crackers and put on our colourful paper hats. As everyone was getting settled, and as Mary was serving the starter course of soup, I was carving the turkey. The sense of excitement was palpable as the great feast of Christmas was getting underway in Aidensfield police house. And then the telephone rang.

I must confess I was tempted to ignore it for I could see the agony in Mary's eyes as we wondered whether it was a call-out, or just a member of our extended family ringing to wish us a happy Christmas. Knowing that I was on duty, I abandoned my turkey duties and went into the office.

'PC Rhea, Aidensfield,' I answered.

'Ah, Nick, sorry if I've disturbed your festivities,' said a rich, masculine, Yorkshire voice. 'Jim Fearnley, Westwood Farm here. But I thought I'd better report this. There's a car in one of my fields. It's run off the road between here and Shelvingby and has rolled down the hillside.'

I knew the road in question. It was a narrow rather winding lane which clung to the side of a lofty hill. The land towered above it at one side, and at the other it fell steeply away. The land in question belonged to Jim Fearnley and comprised a rugged area which was valueless for crops because it sported clumps of gorse and hawthorn in a very rocky terrain. It could be used only by moorland sheep and for grazing hardy cattle.

'It's not icy up there, is it?' I asked, bearing in mind it was the middle of winter.

'No, it's fine and dry. I don't know what happened but it's gone through my fence and must have turned over umpteen times. It's rolled right down the field and come to rest in the hedge at the bottom; it wasn't there when I went down my track half an hour ago to check my sheep and the engine's still warm so it's not been there very long. I've just come past it now so I thought I'd better report it.'

'You did right. Is there anyone with it?' was my obvious question.

'No, not a soul. I can't think where they've gone, no one's been to our house looking for help, and I saw nobody in the village and nobody walking there when I was out just now.'

The road in question led into Shelvingby village, dropping down from the hillside as it did so. Jim's farm gate was about half a mile before reaching the village; the lane leading into his premises began at that point. There was little traffic along there, especially on Christmas Day and I thought it very odd he'd not seen the driver or any passengers. The fact the car had run off the road surely meant there must be a driver nearby. So where had he gone?

'I wonder if it's been stolen?' was my next thought. 'The thief's probably run off. Have you the registration number by any chance? And make?'

'Aye, I thought you might ask that,' and he provided the information. It was a green Ford Anglia about two years old.

'Right, Jim, thanks. I'll check with our office first, just to see if it's been reported stolen, or if the number is known for any reason, then I'll come straight over to have a look at it. I'll be half-an-hour at the most.'

'Aye, right; we'll be in the house if you want us,' and he put down the phone.

When I explained this to Mary, she asked, 'Do you really have to go now, Nick?

Couldn't it wait until after dinner? If there's nobody with it and nobody trapped inside, they must be all right, it's hardly an emergency.'

'That's what's bothering me,' I told her. 'If there was someone with the car, where are they now? Jim's not seen anyone. I'll check to see if it's been stolen.'

When I rang our Sub-Divisional Head-quarters at Eltering and provided them with details of the car, I was told there had been no reports of it being stolen or wanted for any reason. There was no cause to believe it was suspicious in any way. I was tempted to finish my Christmas dinner because there seemed to be no urgency, but some deep instinct told me that things did not seem right. If the car had crashed through a hedge and rolled down a remote hillside, where was the driver? He or she had not been to Westwood Farm seeking help and had not been seen by Jim in Shelvingby village, so what had happened? Jim had been on the scene very soon afterwards and there was nowhere else the driver could have gone, so I couldn't ignore this even if it was a stolen vehicle which had been abandoned by the thief.

'I'll get back as soon as I can,' I told Mary,

as I pushed a piece of turkey into my mouth before heading for my Mini-van. The drive took about twenty-five minutes on empty roads and, as I negotiated the lofty lane towards Shelvingby, I arrived at the gap in the fence. The car had evidently crashed through it at this point, breaking the wooden rails. I stopped and got out to look down the field. There was nothing on the road to suggest why the car had suddenly veered to its right – the surface was in good condition with no ice – but I could see marks in the ground where it had crossed the narrow verge and crashed nose-first into the field, apparently rolling over and over before coming to rest in the hedge at the bottom.

The hedge also bordered Jim's farm track. I drove down the hill and turned into Jim's lane, all the time seeking a dazed or injured person, but saw no one. As I drove along his unsurfaced lane with the farmhouse about half a mile away, the car came into view. It had rolled for several hundred yards so I parked in the nearest gateway and walked into the field.

From a distance, I looked at the car from all angles, hoping this might provide me with some inspiration and then went closer. It was very severely damaged, the result of bouncing down this rough, stony field on its roof and sides. I saw that the front offside tyre had burst – a blow-out? Or the result of rolling down the field? Even now, the engine was still warm and so the accident had happened very recently indeed, probably only minutes before Jim rang me. The driver's door was hanging open too and so I started my search of the interior.

And that's when I found the bag. A woman's handbag. It was tucked under the front passenger seat and in the rear I found a woman's overcoat, a smart black one, along with a small suitcase. I looked in the handbag to see if there was any indication of the owner – being Christmas Day, the Vehicle Taxation Office at County Hall would be closed and so I couldn't call them to check the car number. In the bag among the cosmetics, I found a driving licence in the name of Gloria Jean Holmes with an address in Durham. I could call Durham Police and ask them to call at the address to see if Gloria Jean was at home, or if anyone could throw any light on this matter.

I could do that from my van by radio; I'd call my own headquarters and ask them to contact Durham headquarters with a request that a constable visit her home in an effort to establish where the girl or woman could possibly be. It would all take time and so I took the handbag, case and coat for safe-keeping as I returned to my van to make my calls. And then, as I was walking towards it, I heard a faint cry. It was someone calling for help. It came from somewhere in the gorse bushes, hawthorns and bracken. A woman's cry. I ran to my van, thrust her belongings into it and then raced up the hillside to locate the source of the voice.

'Hello!' I shouted. 'Hello...'

'Help,' came the faint response somewhere to my right.

'I'm coming to find you,' was all I could think of saying. 'Keep shouting to help me...'

I found Gloria Jean. She was a young woman of twenty-two who was badly injured, one leg in particular being at an awkward angle which suggested it was broken. She'd been thrown out of the car during its bouncing journey down the hillside and had, perhaps fortunately, been cast into the side of a gorse bush which had prevented her rolling further down the slope. She'd been unconscious for a time, but had no idea how long; it seemed she'd been on her way to join friends who had rented a country cottage in Shelvingby for Christmas and they hadn't been unduly worried at this stage about her non-arrival. She had no idea what had caused her to drive off the road but said the car had suddenly veered to its right and she'd been unable to stop it. I think the burst tyre was the reason.

I radioed for a doctor and ambulance, remaining with the girl until they arrived, and, as they treated her, I went and told Jim what had happened. He apologized for not searching his field for casualties or even the car for any indication of its owner, but that kind of thing had never occurred to him. It was not the first car to end a journey in one of his fields!

Gloria Jean was whisked off to Ashfordly General Hospital where it was said her condition was not life-threatening. She had been found in time. Her condition could have been very serious if Jim had not found her car so quickly; long exposure on a cold hillside, with a serious injury and the results of shock can cause death in some cases. Although I was invited to join Jim and his family for Christmas dinner, I said I'd better get myself home! My own family would be waiting.

It had taken me over two hours to deal with that fairly minor incident, but I returned to a meal which was still warm in the oven, and just in time for the Queen's speech. I would write up my accident report after Christmas Day and arrange for removal of the vehicle's remains. After telling Mary what had transpired, she realized I could not have ignored that call, whatever its outcome. And as I was enjoying my late dinner, my little son, Charles, came to my side.

'Mummy let me sit in your chair,' he said wisely. 'She said I was man of the house because you weren't here.'

'That's just how it should be,' I smiled, thinking of all those other families out on the moors. That's how they did things, passing responsibility from father to son, mother to daughter, family to family.

As for Gloria Jean and her family, I was so glad I had responded to that call on Christmas Day.

The publishers hope that this book has given you enjoyable reading. Large Print Books are especially designed to be as easy to see and hold as possible. If you wish a complete list of our books please ask at your local library or write directly to:

Magna Large Print Books
Magna House, Long Preston,
Skipton, North Yorkshire.
BD23 4ND

This Large Print Book, for people
who cannot read normal print,
is published under the auspices of

THE ULVERSCROFT FOUNDATION